You're invited to a

CREEPOVER™

Home, Sweet Haunt

written by P. J. Night

SIMON SPOTLIGHT

New York London Toronto Sydney New Delhi

This book is a work of fiction. Any references to historical events, real people, or real places are used fictitiously. Other names, characters, places, and events are products of the author's imagination, and any resemblance to actual events or places or persons, living or dead, is entirely coincidental.

SIMON SPOTLIGHT

An imprint of Simon & Schuster Children's Publishing Division

1230 Avenue of the Americas, New York, New York 10020

Copyright © 2013 by Simon & Schuster, Inc.

All rights reserved, including the right of reproduction in whole or in part in any form.

SIMON SPOTLIGHT and colophon are registered trademarks of Simon & Schuster, Inc.

YOU'RE INVITED TO A CREEPOVER is a trademark of Simon & Schuster, Inc.

Text by Stacia Deutsch

For information about special discounts for bulk purchases, please contact Simon & Schuster Special Sales at 1-866-506-1949 or business@simonandschuster.com.

Manufactured in the United States of America 0713 OFF

First Edition 10 9 8 7 6 5 4 3 2 1

ISBN 978-1-4424-7240-2

ISBN 978-1-4424-7241-9 (eBook)

Library of Congress Control Number 2012951485

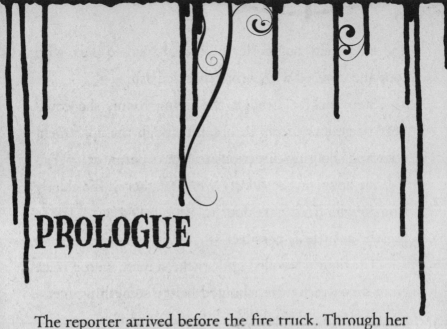

PROLOGUE

The reporter arrived before the fire truck. Through her bedroom window, Nora Wilson saw a woman with long blond hair standing on the sidewalk holding a microphone. A cameraman stood opposite, panning up and down the building as the woman spoke.

Nora couldn't hear what the lady said. All she could do was watch the perfectly dressed, glamorous woman gesture toward the tenth floor and point. Nora waved at the camera, desperately hoping that the fire truck was on its way.

The apartment was hot.

Too hot.

The smoke burned Nora's eyes. It filled her lungs

and made her cough. Her hair was streaked dark with soot and covered with white speckled ash.

"Step back!" Through the living room, she could hear neighbors trying to break through the apartment door and shouting directions to Nora's parents.

"Lie down on the floor!" Mrs. Daugherty, the elderly woman who lived next door in 10G, called out. "Try to breathe as little as possible!"

"The door is swollen and stuck," a man, whose voice Nora didn't recognize, shouted before something metal slammed against the hinges. "It won't open."

A minute later, the sirens arrived and the voices of Nora's neighbors disappeared.

Nora wanted them to stay.

But deep inside, she understood. It wasn't safe. Her neighbors had to leave the building. The firefighters would take over.

The sirens outside whistled and whirred. Inside, a wicked crackling noise echoed through the apartment as the fire spread from the kitchen into the living room.

"On your left!" Nora could hear her father barking orders at her mother as they fought the growing flames with blankets, buckets of water, and a small kitchen fire extinguisher.

Nora didn't have to leave her room to know that anything outside her bedroom door, including the furniture, the TV, the photos and artwork—twelve years of Nora's life—was quickly turning into hot, white ash.

"Nora." Her mother crawled on her belly, like a snake, into the bedroom. Nora's dad slithered along behind her. "Where's Lucas?"

Nora's eight-year-old brother was huddled in a corner of the room, tented under a wet towel. Normally an annoying chatterbox, he hadn't said a word since the fire began.

"The fire is out of control," Nora's dad reported. "We need to stay in here." He shut the bedroom door, dumped a bucket of water on Nora's floral comforter, and stuffed it into the narrow space between the door and the floor. "The fire department will break through the front." He put his hand over Nora's and entwined their fingers. "We'll be fine."

Nora gave her dad a weak smile.

He looked tired. The rims of his eyes were red, and soot covered his hands and face. But he wasn't panicked.

Nora's father and mother were calm about the whole situation. Even her mother, when the oven wiring burst into flames, remained coolly focused. She was a nurse, after all, used to seeing trauma and dealing with emergencies. Her father was an airline pilot who'd flown fighter jets. If they were worried about the fire, they didn't show it. And that kept Nora and Lucas calm as well.

There seemed to be no reason for any of them to be anxious. The firefighters had arrived. Either Nora and her family would soon be downstairs talking to that reporter . . . or . . .

Nora shook off the alternative.

There was nothing left to do but wait.

"Don't open the window," Nora's father warned.

"I know." He'd already told her that there was something called "backdraft." If oxygen entered a sealed room too quickly, there could be a terrible explosion.

Nora rocked onto her knees and stared out at the commotion on the street below. The fire trucks had attached to hydrants. Nora could see the professional men and women wearing heavy black-and-yellow jackets, dragging long gray hoses into the building.

That pretty blond reporter was still there. She wasn't hot and sweating, eyes running, lips parched, covered in smelly ash, barely able to inhale.

No. The reporter still looked gorgeous. Clean white blouse. Straight black skirt. Not one hair out of place.

Nora could see her neighbors gathered on the street. It was early morning, and Mrs. Daugherty was wearing a tattered pink bathrobe with matching fuzzy slippers. Her thin gray hair was rolled in curlers. She was talking to the reporter.

Nora continued to look out the glass, careful not to touch the heated pane.

Backdraft. There was no need for her father to even mention it—Nora couldn't have opened the window if she tried. The lock had been broken, stuck in place, ever since the day her family had moved into the top floor of the ten-story apartment complex.

Her dad had filed a maintenance report. Many maintenance reports.

For twelve years, the property manager had sworn he'd fix it. And the locks on the other windows. And the sticky front door. And the prehistoric oven wiring . . .

CHAPTER 1

TWO MONTHS LATER

Nora used to have a normal life. It was so normal it was boring. She went to school, did her homework, hung out with her friends, had dinner with her family, and avoided her irritating younger brother.

That was before. Before the fire swept through their apartment and her parents changed into nervous freaks.

The fire was in late August. When the school year started in September, her parents wouldn't let her or Lucas out of the apartment. Seriously. Not even into the hallway.

They wanted to be with Nora and Lucas all the time. Protect them from the world. Nora's parents, who had never been afraid of anything, were suddenly afraid to let their children out of their sight.

For weeks after the fire, Nora insisted that "lightning doesn't strike the same place twice," but her parents said she was wrong.

Her father understood weather patterns. He told Nora that the Empire State Building was hit by lightning as many as one hundred times each year. Her mother was frantic with worry that something bad might happen again.

Nora tried everything she could think of to convince them they were being overprotective. But they wouldn't bend.

Her mother quit her job to homeschool them. Her father quit his job to stay at home as well. They disconnected the Internet. Never replaced the TV, cell phones, or computers that had melted in the flames. Their furniture was charred and all their clothing smelled like barbecue. It didn't matter how many times the shirts and pants were washed.

Nora longed for the old kind of normal. She wished things would go back to the old kind of boring. She'd never complain again.

"Pssst." Lucas stuck his shaggy brown head into Nora's bedroom. He was wearing pajama pants and a matching shirt. "Whatcha doing?"

Nora sighed. Before the fire her brother had bugged her, but at least she hadn't had to spend all day, every day, with him.

It was on Nora's tongue to say *None of your business* and toss Lucas out of her room, but she knew that the fire and everything after had been hard for him, too.

Before, Lucas had been creative, adventurous, and an expert at talking his way out of trouble. Stuck in the apartment, Lucas had no use for his skills. With nowhere to go and not much to do, he channeled all his energy into annoying Nora.

Unfortunately, Lucas had a lot of energy to channel.

Her mother told Nora to be nice.

It was hard, super hard, but since she didn't have any one else to hang out with, she tried her best.

Instead of booting her brother out of the room, Nora moved over on the bed to let Lucas sit next to her. In exchange for promising her parents that she'd be nice, Nora had gotten permission to push her bed over by the window. The lock still didn't open, but at least she could look outside. There were a few shops and a park across the street.

Lucas piled Nora's pillows so that he could lie down and look outside at the same time. "Still staring out the window every morning?" her brother asked.

"And afternoon," Nora said.

"You never give up, do you?"

That wasn't really a question, so Nora didn't reply. It was 7:37. Three more minutes. She didn't want to miss seeing her friends. This was the only way.

A few days after the fire, Nora had tried calling them on the only phone (cell or otherwise) that wasn't destroyed in the fire—the one in her parents' bedroom—but the connection was always bad. Although she could hear them perfectly, they could never hear her. Figuring the heat from the flames had melted the wiring, Nora asked her parents to contact the telephone company. That was around the time they called a "family meeting" to announce that they were both quitting their jobs, staying at home, and letting the less important bills lapse. They could no longer afford phones, Internet, and cable TV.

"I have to try," Nora told Lucas. "Maybe if Hallie and Lindsay finally look up at my window, they will see me and come over. There's no way my friends could have forgotten me already."

Seven thirty-eight. She couldn't be distracted. "You can stay here," she told Lucas, "but no talking."

Lucas said, "Even if they did see you, Mom and Dad would never—"

Nora whipped her head around and shot him an evil look. "Shhhh." She put a finger to her lips.

Lucas changed the subject. "Forget about them. We can have an adventure together today. I found this really great—"

"Quiet!" Nora hissed, interrupting him for the second time. "I *have* to pay attention." Just past the park was an apartment building much like Nora's. The exterior had the same old-fashioned classic brickwork, but the inside had been renovated. None of their windows were stuck shut, and all their wiring worked.

Hallie and Lindsay lived in that building. In apartments on the same floor, next door to each other.

Nora had only one minute twenty-three seconds to get their attention. That was how long it took them to leave the building, walk by the park, and turn the corner toward school.

Today was the day they'd look up.

Nora could feel it in her bones.

Halloween had always been their favorite holiday. The three of them had celebrated it together every year since kindergarten. They played pranks on each other; every Halloween was a competition to see who could get the biggest scream. There was the annual haunted house at the recreation center and then they'd all go trick-or-treating in Hallie and Lindsay's building. The night would end with a sleepover at Hallie's apartment and an all-night scary movie marathon. Tonight was the first time Nora wouldn't be there.

Chatting about costumes and candy would definitely make Hallie and Lindsay think of her. They'd both tilt their heads and glance at her window.

It was going to happen. Nora was sure. And she'd be there to wave to them.

"I'm just saying," Lucas began again, "when the fire department came, they used the old plans to the apartment building like a map. They left the blueprints here. There's a—"

"SHHHH," Nora commanded.

Forty-two seconds until Hallie and Lindsay would be

on the street. She raised her hand and held it flat against the pane. Nora was ready to start waving.

"Your room used to be a butler's pantry room." Lucas stared at the side of Nora's face. "Did you know that? These apartments were built to have servants who cooked and cleaned! The kids never had to do chores." Lucas tried to get her attention as he said, "All your baby animal and band posters cover the original wallpaper."

"Whatever." Nora didn't care. She refused to look at him. Lucas continued yammering, but Nora stopped listening. Completely focused on the street below her window, she saw the shadows of her friends darken the sidewalk before she saw them in person.

"Hallie Malik!" Nora screamed at the top of her voice. She waved both her arms wildly. "Lindsay Sanchez! Up here!"

They didn't tip their heads.

The glass pane was thin. Several cracks had formed from the fire. It wasn't much of a barrier.

If she listened really closely, Nora could hear *them* talking about Kyle Murphy, a boy in their school. So why couldn't they hear *her* shouting their names like a maniac?

Nora noticed that Hallie was wearing a costume to school. In fact, as the girls stepped into the sunlight, Nora could see that both girls were wearing the outfits they'd all picked out together back in July.

Leggings and neon-colored lace tank tops. High-heeled shoes and teased-up hair. They were pop stars. This was so unfair.

Nora was supposed to be the third of their musical trio. They were going to lip-sync to their favorite song at the Halloween party at school.

To complete their outfits, the two girls were wearing matching yellow jackets with hand-embroidered flowers down the back and along one sleeve. Lindsay had found them in a small shop when she went to visit her grand-mother in Mexico. She'd texted back pictures, and Nora and Hallie agreed they were perfect.

Lindsay was supposed to bring back three, but after the fire, she never stopped by to drop off Nora's jacket.

"Hey, did you get *me* a jacket?" Nora shouted toward the street below. "I'll wear mine, too. Just bring it over!"

She leaned toward the windowpane, screaming "Hey!" and "Hello!" and the girls' names over and over. But they didn't react.

"It's Halloween!" Nora shrieked. "Remember?! Remember me?!"

In frustration Nora clenched her hands into fists, when Lucas suddenly reached out and grabbed both Nora's arms.

"No!" he shouted at her, pulling her arms down. "Don't!"

"I only have a few more seconds." Nora yanked her hands out of his. "They're crossing in front of our apartment building."

"But the glass." Lucas dove on top of Nora, pinning her arms to the bed. "It's weak."

He was smaller than she was. Nora easily rolled him off of her and pushed past him. She pointed one hand at the door while preparing to smack the glass with her other. "I'm only going to make a loud noise."

"It'll shatter!" Lucas screamed at the same time Nora yelled, "Get out of my way!" She kicked him hard in the shin. Lucas grabbed his leg. "Ow!"

Nora knew he wasn't really hurt. Lucas had always been an excellent actor.

While Lucas made a show of rolling around and groaning, Nora bolted forward. Peeking out the window, she could see that the girls had already passed the park. Thirteen seconds until they disappeared from sight. This was it. This was her chance.

"No!!!" Lucas screamed, grabbing his sister around the waist.

Nora pushed him away with her bare feet and popped up behind the window frame. She gave the glass a huge banging pound with both fists simultaneously.

The banging sound was loud like Nora had hoped. And, just like Lucas said it would, the glass also crumbled into a million little pieces.

Nora did a quick check of her arms. No shards of glass stuck in them. No scratches either. Nora took advantage of the broken window.

"Hallie! Lindsay!" Nora leaned out the empty frame to see them looking up toward her broken bedroom window. Nora finally had their attention. "Happy Halloween!" she called down.

Hallie looked at Lindsay, eyes wide.

Lindsay glanced at the window, then at Hallie. Her mouth hung open in a perfect O.

Nora raised her hands above her head. "Come over later! Trick-or-treat in my building tonight! I'll ask my parents. I'm sure they'll let me go with—" She lost her balance. "Aughhhhh!" Nora flailed as she fell forward and farther out the window.

Lucas grabbed Nora around the waist and pulled her back an instant before she fell, ten stories to the pavement below.

"No, no, no! Let go of me!" Nora kicked him in the shin and tore out of his arms. She peered out the window frame.

The street was empty.

Her friends were gone.

Nora spun on her brother, who was sitting on the edge of her bed holding his leg. "Get out of my room. Get out and never come back!"

"I saved your life." Lucas stood up, leaning on his left leg. "You could have fallen out the window. You should be thanking me."

"They didn't answer me!" Nora screamed. "They won't come over for trick-or-treating, and I'll never convince Mom and Dad to let me go out with them. No candy. No scary stories. Halloween is ruined! It's all your fault!" She threw a pillow off the bed at Lucas's head. He ducked and she missed. By a mile.

Her terrible throw made Lucas laugh. He laughed so hard tears filled his eyes. When Nora scooped up a second pillow and tossed it again, he stuck out his tongue before dodging her throw.

"WAR!" Nora declared. She leaped on her brother and wrestled him to the ground.

He was small, but quick.

Lucas managed to roll away from Nora, swooping a pillow off the floor as he made his escape. With a wallop, he hit her soundly in the side of the head.

"Ooof!" Nora grunted, grabbing the other pillow and swinging it back at Lucas with all her might.

Direct hit. The pillow smacked Lucas square in the chest, throwing him backward. The seam burst open. Nora dove forward, hitting him over and over again with the torn pillow until feathers were everywhere.

Lucas chuckled as he hit her again with his own pillow. That pillow also ripped, and more feathers poured into the room.

Back and forth they went, swinging at each other until the pillowcases were empty. Then they started throwing handfuls of feathers at each other.

"I win!" Nora exclaimed, holding her brother's arms

behind his back. "And now you will suffer."

"You did not win! I did!" Lucas giggled. With a mighty shove, he tipped her over and tried to hold her firm.

"This isn't funny." Nora was struggling against his grasp when their mother walked into the room.

"What is going on here?" Nora's mother glanced around before calling, "Frank!" to her husband down the hall.

"Laura, I—" Mr. Wilson began as he reached Nora's bedroom. His voice dropped. "Whoa."

Nora and Lucas were wrapped together on the floor, a tangled mess of arms and legs.

The room was covered with white feathers. It looked like it had snowed.

The window was broken.

And shattered glass covered Nora's bed.

CHAPTER 2

When the mess was cleaned up, Lucas and Nora were both sent to shower. Then they had a "family meeting" in the living room. This was the second formal meeting ever in Wilson family history. The first one had been a few days after the fire. That meeting changed her life. Nora expected this one to be bad as well.

Nora sat back into the couch. The fabric had once been soft velvet, but velvet burned easily. Rough towels covered the holes, and the floppy cushions were held together with duct tape. The sofa smelled like burnt toast.

Lucas came in. His hair was wet and he was wearing shorts and a T-shirt. Lucas stomped across the floor as usual. He was the loudest walker in the world. Nora always wondered why the people who lived below never complained. After all, in an apartment building, their floor was someone's ceiling.

"That was fun today," Lucas whispered to Nora. He took one last clumping step toward the couch. "We need to have more fun."

Nora sneered at him.

"About our adventure—" Lucas began.

"Sit!" Mr. Wilson interrupted. He directed Lucas to the space next to Nora on the sofa.

Nora prepared herself to be punished. Although she had to wonder what more could be taken away from her.

"After what happened this morning, it has occurred to us that you've both gotten a little stir-crazy," Mrs. Wilson said, tilting her head at the kids.

"So we've decided to let you go outside," Nora's father put in. "Run around and blow off some steam."

"We aren't in trouble?" Nora bolted up to her feet. At her father's strong stare she plopped back onto the couch, feeling the springs settle beneath her weight. Perhaps the day wasn't ruined after all.

"You'll need to do extra chores," her mother said. "And an extra math assignment."

Nora groaned.

"Does Lucas get extra math?" Nora asked.

"No," her mother said. "He's younger than you, Nora. You should have known better than to fight with him."

"He started it," Nora complained, but then let the argument drop as she realized they'd said something more important. She had to be sure she'd heard right. "Wait, did you say we *can* go *out* of the apartment?" Nora would gladly do a million math assignments for an afternoon in the sun and a chance to see her friends.

"It's Halloween," her father said, as if Nora hadn't already known. "A special occasion."

"Yeah . . ." She wanted them to hurry to the going outside part.

"You can go to the park," her father added, squashing Nora's plans to rush over to school and see all her old friends. Nora strained to hear when he turned to her mother and said in a whisper, "Mrs. Daugherty's living room window faces away from the park. It'll be fine as long as they hurry across the hall and avoid hanging around waiting for the elevator." He glared at Nora and said in a louder voice, "Use the stairs."

"Stairs?" But there were so many. Nora began to

complain, when her mother pinned her with a stern look.

"We will watch you from here." Their own living room window looked out directly at the park. Her mother's voice was hard. "You may not go anywhere else." She lowered her eyes at Nora and didn't blink.

Ugh.

Going to the park was so babyish. There were swings and a slide designed for kids half her age. Then again, the park was better than nothing at all. Plus, if she thought about it really hard, Nora was certain she could figure out a way to get Hallie and Lindsay to hang out with her there. She'd need a plan, that was all.

"Okay." Again Nora began to get off the couch.

Her father stopped her escape. "You'll go today from noon to three."

Nora slumped back down. "But school isn't out until three," she whined. "Hallie and Lindsay don't come around the corner until twelve minutes after! With that rule, I won't see them."

Mrs. Wilson shrugged. "It's for the best," she said, flashing a glance at Nora's dad.

"That's the deal," her father said. "Take it or leave it."

"Hmmm." Nora exhaled sharply. It wasn't like her

to break rules; that was Lucas's thing. But maybe, just this once, Nora could stay out an extra fifteen minutes. She'd do two million math problems for the chance to see her friends.

"I'm not finished," Mr. Wilson said. "Nora, you have to take Lucas with you."

"We can't go today." Lucas grinned. "We're going to have a Halloween adventure right here in the building."

"No, we're not," Nora said, frowning. The only adventure she was going to have was outside. With her friends. Hanging with Lucas was not part of the plan.

"I saved your life," Lucas countered. "You owe me."

Nora groaned. "I wasn't going to fall out the window."

"Yes, you were," Lucas began.

Mrs. Wilson put up a hand to stop the argument before it began. She said, "Your father already told you the deal, Nora. Now you can decide if you want to go or not."

Nora stared at her parents for a long moment.

"Oh, fine," she said at last. "I'll take the pest to the park." She glared at Lucas and wondered how hard it would be to ditch him. With the way he'd been lately, probably impossible.

"You better be ready to go out at noon. Not

noon-oh-one. Don't be late," Nora told her brother.

Without waiting for his response, Nora ran into her room to pick what she'd wear. A costume? Jeans? T-shirt? This was so exciting.

"Huh?" She stopped in her doorway.

Her parents had nailed a thick wooden board over the broken glass. They must have done it while she showered.

Nora couldn't see outside anymore.

They'd also moved her bed back to the center of the room.

"Bummer," Nora muttered as she began flipping through her clothes.

Not having the same jacket as Hallie and Lindsay was yet another bummer. She picked black leggings and a lacy hot-pink tank top. Tying her hair up in a high ponytail, Nora did her best to match Hallie's and Lindsay's costumes.

"You look great," Mrs. Wilson said when Nora walked into the living room. "A rock star."

"Pop star," Nora corrected.

"Oh, right," her mother said with a smile. "My mistake."

"I'm ready," Nora told her. "Where's Lucas?"

"In his room." Mr. Wilson pointed down the hall. "Go get him."

Just to let them know how she felt about being her brother's escort, Nora huffed.

"I'll be watching," her mother said, indicating she was going to watch from the living room window. "Don't leave the park."

"Got it. Got it," Nora repeated impatiently before stomping down the hallway. "Lucas?" Nora went to his room and opened the door.

He wasn't there.

She checked the bathroom and the hallway and her parents' room.

It wasn't like the apartment was so big. He had to be somewhere!

"Lucas!" Nora shouted his name as she wandered around looking in all the rooms again. Even her room was empty.

She felt her blood starting to rise into her cheeks. Where was he?!

Back in Lucas's room, she found a note lying on his bed. It read: *Happy Halloween.* Then below that he'd drawn a picture of a cartoon ghost with a comic bubble over his head that said: *Boo!*

Nora groaned. She'd made it clear she didn't want to have an adventure with him.

"I'm leaving," she called out, in case Lucas was hiding somewhere.

No reply. Only silence.

"Have fun by yourself," she called into the air. Then, "See ya later."

Nora checked the clock. It was 12:05 now. Her freedom was ticking away. She rushed into the kitchen.

"Mom," she said, "Lucas doesn't want to come with me." That was true enough.

"I suppose you can go alone," her mother said, checking with her father for confirmation. He nodded. "Hurry to the stairs."

Waving good-bye to her parents, Nora opened the door to the apartment, and for the first time in what felt like forever, stepped into the floral-carpeted hallway.

The park was quiet. All the kids were at school. The brightly colored hard plastic equipment was fun when

Nora was little. The red slide seemed so tall then. Now Nora could easily reach up and touch the top platform. The slide was attached to yellow climbing cubes, which led to the blue-and-green monkey bars.

Over to the side, across a sandy patch, two thick black rubber swings hung from chains attached to a purple-painted metal rod. A toddler's swing, one of those seats with leg holes, was in the third space, nearest the slide.

Nora went down the slide a few times before camping out on a swing. She opened the book she had brought with her, but she had trouble concentrating on the words.

It didn't take long to realize that the park would be way more fun with friends.

By the end of the first hour, Nora sort of even wished that Lucas would show up. Sort of.

Dragging her feet in the sand, Nora raised her chin up to feel the afternoon sun on her face. It was warm, but the air was crisp. A typical autumn day. It had been a long time since she'd been in the sun at all. Maybe she should have put on sunscreen. She was surprised her mother hadn't insisted.

Nora was daydreaming, thinking of how she was going survive the next two hours, clever ways to greet her friends, and what excuses she'd give her mom when she got back to the apartment after three o'clock, when she heard voices around the corner. Raising her head, Nora tipped her ear to be sure. Yep! Nora recognized those voices!

With everything that had happened, she'd forgotten that today was an early dismissal from school. School let out at one fifteen on Halloween!

This was awesome. Nora was going to see her friends without getting in any trouble when she returned home.

Fast as lightning, Nora jumped off the swing and dashed behind some nearby bushes.

It was going to be an amazing surprise. She was going to jump out and hug Hallie first, since she'd known her longer. Nora had met Hallie the first day of kindergarten. They hadn't met Lindsay until the second day.

Then she considered that since she talked more often at night to Lindsay, maybe she should hug her first.

Or should it be a group hug?

Nora still hadn't decided whom she was going to hug first when the two girls approached the bush where she was hiding. She held her breath until they passed. Nora sucked her cheeks together and tried not to make even a single little peeping sound.

"So what time should we meet for trick-or-treating?" Hallie asked Lindsay.

"Seven," Lindsay replied.

"I'm sad to go without Nora," Hallie said.

Nora knew it. They hadn't forgotten her!

"Freaky, what happened this morning," Lindsay said.

Hallie pulled her pop-star jacket tightly around herself and shook her head.

Lindsay put her arm around Hallie. "I think we should agree not to mention it ever again."

Of course. Now Nora understood what had happened. Popping up and down in the window frame as she fought with Lucas had made them uncertain if they'd really seen her or not. She wished she'd planned it on purpose. It fit in with the theme of the day!

Well then, how about another fright?

It would be the perfect way to surprise her friends. Forget the hugs. They loved being scared. All those movies they'd watched together while sleeping at Hallie's on Halloween night. All those pranks they'd pulled on one another. This was going to be the ultimate. Hallie and Lindsay would be frightened for a moment, and then they'd laugh when they realized it was her. It would be just like old times.

Nora grinned.

As Hallie and Lindsay passed by the bushes, Nora tiptoed out of her hiding place. She crept up slowly, careful not to let them see her before she was ready.

The girls slowed down at the edge of the park. Nora wasn't allowed to go any farther, and she knew her mother was watching, so she had to act now. An inch at a time, she reached her hand out to touch Hallie on the shoulder.

"Boo!" she shouted as Hallie turned.

"Ahhhh!" Hallie screamed in Nora's face. Her breath smelled like cafeteria pizza.

Nora rested her hand on Lindsay's shoulder and said, "Surprise!"

"AHHHHHHH!" Lindsay's shrieks practically broke Nora's eardrums.

"Ha-ha!" Nora giggled. "I got you guys good!"

The two girls grabbed hands with each other and ran the last few feet to their apartment building. Nora could see their eyes bulging out of their pale faces as they took one last look behind them before slamming the door shut.

"Wait!" Nora rushed after Hallie and Lindsay. "Wait for me!" There must have been something scary behind her for Hallie and Lindsay to have run like that. Nora timidly glanced over her shoulder, expecting to see someone in a realistic, horrifying costume: maybe an eerie horseman carrying his severed head under one arm or a blood-soaked werewolf with soggy guts hanging from his snarling jaws.

She didn't see anyone right away. But whoever it was could be hiding again. Like she had. There was a row of trees a few feet behind her. The person must be preparing to pop out and give Nora the fright of her life. Although she knew she'd be busted by her parents for leaving the park, Nora decided she didn't care. Afraid of whatever was lurking behind her, she rushed to Hallie and Lindsay's apartment complex and tugged on the door. It was locked.

She pressed the buzzer for Hallie's apartment. Then buzzed Lindsay's.

They didn't answer.

Nora kept pressing the buttons, figuring they'd pick up. But no one did. She swallowed her nerves and let out her breath in one huge gust. Whatever was out there, she'd have to face it, alone. Steeling her courage, Nora turned and started walking back to the park.

CHAPTER 3

A few moments later Nora entered the row of trees. She walked as silently as she could while she looked behind every one. She even looked inside a bush, but there was no one.

Maybe this was Hallie and Lindsay's Halloween trick on Nora?

They must have pretended to be scared and then run away from her.

That made sense. Nora had done something similar in second grade. It was hysterical when they were seven. But now they were older, and after five minutes of leaning on their apartment buzzers, Nora had to admit that the joke was no longer funny.

Nora went back to the park swings and sat down. She wondered what had gone wrong.

Nora had thought her friends would be happy to see her. She'd assumed they'd all hang out and have a great Halloween, just like old times. Nora was now sure of what she hadn't wanted to admit: At best, Hallie and Lindsay didn't want to be friends with her because she wasn't allowed out of her apartment. At worst, they had forgotten about her completely.

It was almost two o'clock, and Nora didn't know what to do. She didn't want to be in the park alone for another hour. Going home seemed like a terrible idea since she didn't know when she'd *ever* be let outside again. It would be a mistake to stand on the doorstep of Hallie and Lindsay's apartment building and ring the buzzer another million times. They weren't coming out.

Nora could feel *that* in her bones.

"Hi."

Nora looked up to see a girl her own age looking down at her and smiling. The girl had dark skin with golden eyes and sporty short hair.

"I'm Caitlin," the girl said. "Are you new around here?"

"No." Nora pinched her lips together and quickly added, "I just don't get out much."

"Oh." Caitlin sat down on the empty swing next to Nora and spun around, twisting the chain. "Well, I'm new." She let the chain go and the swing spun around twice before stopping. Caitlin twisted it up and let go again. "I moved to the neighborhood last month," she said.

"What school do you go to?" Nora asked.

"Westside." Caitlin said the name of Nora's old school.

"Oh," Nora said, perking up. "Do you know Hallie Malik and Lindsay Sanchez?" Maybe Caitlin could get them to answer the bell, and Nora could start the afternoon over.

"Nope," Caitlin said as she considered the names. "It's a big school. I don't know many people yet."

"I see." Nora frowned.

"Where do you go?" Caitlin asked.

"I used to go to Westside, but I'm homeschooled now," Nora said.

"That explains why you don't get out much," Caitlin replied. She sat thoughtfully for a long silent moment before asking, "Do you like it? Homeschooling?"

"I don't have a choice," Nora replied simply.

"Oh," Caitlin said.

The conversation faded again before Caitlin asked, "Want to see who can swing highest?"

"Sure." Nora used to be able to go the highest of her friends. Her ex-friends.

The girls took turns pumping their legs and soaring. Nora was higher than Caitlin when suddenly, at the top of the arc, Caitlin leaped off her seat. She made a perfect landing, arms raised, in the grass beyond the sandbox.

"Awesome!" Nora tried to do the same thing. Her landing wasn't nearly as smooth, and she tumbled, rolling on the soft lawn.

"Nice crash." Caitlin laughed. She turned a couple cartwheels before executing a backflip. "I probably should have warned you that I take gymnastics."

Nora stretched out on the grass and looked up at the sky. "I bet you're really good," Nora said.

Flopping down next to Nora, Caitlin replied, "I practice a lot. I don't have many friends at school because I'm at the gym so much. I do tumbling and floor before school every day and vault and beam after."

Nora had never been committed to just one thing. Before, when she was allowed to leave the apartment building, Nora had taken a few months of dance and several tennis lessons. She'd tried theater, yearbook, and soccer at school. There wasn't any activity she had liked enough to decide to dedicate her life to it.

"You should be in the Olympics!" she told Caitlin.

"That's my goal," Caitlin said. "I really love gymnastics."

Nora was impressed. Caitlin was following her dreams. Nora wondered what her own dreams were. She didn't really have any idea what she wanted to be when she grew up. She was already twelve years old. Almost a teenager.

When Nora got back to the apartment, she was going to start thinking about what she liked and what she wanted to do. She must be really good at *something*, but what?

"Come on. Let's go." Caitlin popped up and raced to the slide.

The depressing image Nora had had of living friend-less forever in the barbecue-smelling apartment with Lucas faded away, and a fresh surge of hope took its place.

"I'm in," Nora said happily.

From the slides to the monkey bars, to somersaults on the lawn, then to the swings again, Caitlin was in constant motion. Nora followed her through the park, sweating and panting, and having a terrific time.

"I'm so glad we met," Caitlin said as the two girls began to swing again.

"Me too," Nora said. It was nearly three o'clock. She had to leave. Bummer. Nora wished they had more time to get to know each other better.

As if she'd read Nora's mind, Caitlin said, "Two of my friends from the gymnastics studio are coming for trick-or-treating tonight. Do you want to come with us?"

Nora glanced across the street to her apartment building, then let her eyes travel up to the top floor. She could see the shadow of her mother staring out through the glass.

"Come on, Nora. It'll be fun!" Caitlin said. She noticed where Nora was looking and asked, "Do you live in that building?" Caitlin pointed across the park.

"Yes," Nora replied as her mother waved for her to come in.

"Fab-u-lous!" Caitlin cheered, leaping off the swing,

turning herself around in the air like a tornado before landing. "That's where I live too."

"You do?" There weren't many other kids in the building, and Nora didn't know any of them. In fact, Nora didn't really know anyone who lived in her building except for Mrs. Daugherty, who had lived next door to the Wilsons for Nora's entire life. People were always moving in and out, and she was always over at Hallie and Lindsay's. It was so cool that someone her age had moved in!

"Second floor," Caitlin replied. "So can you come? You already have an awesome pop-star costume." She added, "I'm going to be a zombie."

Slowing to a stop, Nora chose to step off the swing instead of jump. She was eager to talk to her parents about letting her do more stuff, but didn't think it would happen right away. Even before the fire, they were slow to change their minds after they'd made a decision.

It took two months and a really big pillow fight to get permission to go outside. Nora didn't have another two months to convince them to let her trick-or-treat with Caitlin and her friends.

"There's no way," Nora groaned. "My parents like

me to stay close to home." *Like, so close I don't leave the apartment.*

"Your parents are superprotective, huh?" Caitlin asked.

"Yeah," Nora replied.

"How 'bout this?" She had a suggestion. "Tell them that we won't leave the building. We can trick-or-treat at the neighbors' and then sleep over at my apartment. Do you like ghost stories?"

"Yes!" Nora said, nodding eagerly. "I love them."

Caitlin glanced around, then whispered, "I hear our building is haunted."

"Really?" Nora's eyes went wide. She'd never heard that! If she had, every year Nora would have insisted that she, Hallie, and Lindsay go trick-or-treating and sleep at her place instead of Hallie's. It was a well-known fact that ghosts come out on Halloween. Movie ghosts were not nearly as terrifying as real ones! Not even close.

"I really want to come," Nora said, bouncing on her toes. She could see her mom waving both hands now at her through the window. Time was up.

"Ask your parents," Caitlin said. "I'm in apartment 2H."

"I'll try," Nora said. She crossed her fingers that her parents would agree.

They left the park together and entered their apartment building.

Nora had walked down the stairs like her parents had told her to, but she didn't see anything wrong with taking the elevator back up. She wanted to stick with Caitlin as long as possible.

"I'm going to go get changed into my costume," Caitlin said as the elevator door opened. "Don't get too scared when you see me!"

"I'll try not to freak out." Nora giggled.

Caitlin got off the elevator at the second floor. Nora pushed the button for the tenth.

"Don't forget to say hi to the ghost as you go up," Caitlin told Nora.

"Where does he live?" Nora asked.

"Ninth floor," Caitlin said. "Beware of 9G!" She moaned like a ghost. "Oooooh. Oooooh."

The sound echoed in the elevator shaft and followed Nora the rest of the way home.

CHAPTER 4

"I made a new friend at the park. We're the same age and she's nice and she's a gymnast and she invited me—"

Nora's dad looked up from the book he was reading. He was sitting on the couch, wearing a red shirt the same color as the velvet. Nora hadn't seen him there when she first dashed through the door. Her whole speech had been directed at her mother, who was still by the window, looking down toward the street.

"You talked to someone?" Her father sounded interested.

"Yes," Nora said. She started the whole explanation again. She'd said it all fast the first time, and was speaking even faster this round. "We're the same age and she's—"

"Got it." Her dad scooted over to make room for Nora.

"Did you get the invitation part?" Nora asked, since that was where she'd stopped the first time through. She took the seat.

"Yes," her father said, setting his book aside and giving Nora his full attention.

Nora's mother came over to the couch. There wasn't any other furniture in the room. The coffee table and the old rocking chair had both been destroyed in the fire. Since the Wilsons didn't have the money to replace anything, she sat on the floor near Nora's feet.

Nora began to stand, to trade places with her mom, but Mrs. Wilson motioned for her to sit back down.

"So can I?" Nora asked as she moved slightly to the left. An exposed spring was poking her in the thigh. "Can I go?"

"I saw Hallie and Lindsay come by the park," Nora's mom said without answering.

Nora had forgotten her mom had been in the window the whole time she'd been away.

"Did you see what happened?" she asked. A rosy flush settled in Nora's cheeks. She was embarrassed by how they'd treated her. And mad. Her cheeks felt warm and tight. Nora let out a big breath.

"No. Lucas needed help. I had to show him how to tie strong knots," Mrs. Wilson said. "When I got back, I noticed that you were sitting alone on a swing." She paused, then asked, "Do you want to talk about it?"

Nora shook her head. "They weren't very happy to see me."

"Okay." Mrs. Wilson faced Nora's dad. "Maybe we should—"

"Let me go to the sleepover?" Nora finished her mother's sentence.

"Nora, don't interrupt," her father scolded.

"I'm sorry," she said, putting a hand on her own knee to keep it from bouncing. "I'm just superexcited about Caitlin's."

"Hmmm." Mr. Wilson gave his wife a long look. "It *is* Halloween."

"I know! That's the reason for the . . ." Nora bit her tongue. She was interrupting again. "Sorry."

"I've read that the veil is thinner," Mrs. Wilson told Nora's dad.

Veil? Were they talking about weddings? Nora didn't

know and, having been busted twice for interrupting, decided not to ask. She needed to be on her best behavior if she wanted to convince them to let her go.

There was a look in her mother's eyes that Nora couldn't identify. She felt like she was eavesdropping on a private conversation.

"I didn't really believe it was possible," Nora's dad said. "Using the stairs today was a precaution, just in case. But now it seems like maybe . . ."

"The facts are clear: Two were shocked. One has no clue." Nora's mother ran a hand through her hair before stating, "I don't think this is a good idea, Frank."

Nora didn't get the first part of the conversation, but the "not a good idea" part she got. When the conversation fell to a pause and Nora was certain she wasn't interrupting, she made her case.

"Caitlin lives in our building. On the second floor. Her friends from gymnastics are coming too. We'll stick together, and she promised we won't go outside." Her words were tumbling out so fast Nora could barely keep up with herself. "I can't stay locked in this apartment forever."

"We don't keep you inside to torture you, Nora."

Nora's mother was defensive, and Nora wondered if she'd said the wrong thing.

"We have our reasons, Nora," her father said. "Adult reasons that might be hard for you to understand."

"Please," Nora whined. She wanted to go to Caitlin's so, so, so badly.

"I still wonder if—" Nora's mother began, when Lucas clumped like Bigfoot into the room.

"What are you talking about?" he asked.

How was it that if Lucas interrupted, no one said anything? Typical. Unfair.

"Nora's been invited to a friend's apartment for trick-or-treating and a sleepover tonight," Nora's mother explained.

"A sleepover?" Lucas asked. He rotated on his heel to face Nora. "You can't go. I'm planning a big adventure."

"I already told you. I'm not going on any adventures with you," Nora grumbled.

While Nora's parents spoke in low voices, Lucas leaned in close to Nora and said, "I discovered the most incredible, amazing thing. You are going to *love* it."

"No. I won't. I won't even *like* it," Nora said. Then she had an idea. Lucas was the one who could convince their parents of anything. He was the one who never got punished. "Hey," she said, "if you help me get to the sleepover, I will . . ." She paused before going on. It was like swallowing nails. With a deep sigh, she said, "I'll hang out with you. Do whatever you want." She quickly added, "Tomorrow."

"But tomorrow's not Halloween." Lucas pinched his lips as he considered her offer. "It's a Halloween type of adventure."

"I want to go to Caitlin's tonight," Nora said. "Whatever you've got planned can wait."

Lucas continued to think about it. "Caitlin's, huh?" A glimmer came into his eyes that made Nora uneasy. He was up to something. "What apartment does she live in?"

She tried to ignore her suspicions. "2H."

Lucas was thinking so hard, his lips were moving. Nora tried to read whatever was passing through his brain, but couldn't make out anything specific.

"Okay," he said at last. "You've got a deal." He stuck out his hand for a shake.

As she took his clammy hand in hers, Nora wasn't sure exactly what she'd agreed to.

Lucas gave Nora a wink, then interrupted their parents again, saying, "Mom. Dad."

They both turned. Neither told him to wait. Or to go to his room.

"I think it's a great idea for Nora to go to Caitlin's tonight." Lucas sounded older than eight as he explained. "Nora sits in the window every day, hoping her old friends will look up at her." He was on a roll. Very serious, as if he were a professional therapist. "She has a classic case of Post-Traumatic Fire Disorder. PTFD." If their parents knew Lucas had made up his diagnosis, they didn't comment. Instead they let him go on, without cracking a smile.

Nora was holding back laughter. Lucas was a creative storyteller. He could instantly invent stuff that sounded perfectly true. PTFD. Ha! No wonder he never got in trouble.

"Nora is stuck in the days before the fire, unable to focus on the future."

Actually, that did sound like what she had. If it was a real psychological state, then they all had it.

"The only cure is for Nora to make new friends." Lucas finished his speech.

Nora was ready to jump up off the sofa and give Lucas a standing ovation. She had to admit, her brother was truly an excellent actor. Riveted by his performance, Nora stayed in her seat, waiting for her parents' reaction.

The only thing Nora would have added to Lucas's argument was that she didn't only need new friends, but she also needed to get out and try new things: photography, music lessons, swimming, maybe even gymnastics. If she wanted to find out what she was good at and pursue it, then she had to try everything! Nora considered that maybe Lucas could teach her a few things about acting.

Her parents put their heads together to discuss their decision.

"I suppose it would be all right," her father said loud enough for Nora to overhear.

"I don't know." Her mother's voice was softer, and Nora couldn't hear anything else.

They went back and forth a few times, and Nora grew nervous.

"Don't worry," Lucas told her. "I'm very good. Convincing is my specialty."

Nora crossed her fingers and hoped he was right.

"Nora," her father said at last. "Your mother and I agree, you may go to trick-or-treating."

"Yes!" Nora threw herself into his arms. "Can I use the elevator to get there?"

"I suppose that would be okay," her father said. "But you cannot sleep over. You have to be home by ten p.m."

Nora pulled back. "Please, please, please," she whined.

"That's the deal." Her mother echoed her father's earlier words. "Take it or leave it."

"I'll take it!" Nora said. Her parents weren't going to give her everything she wanted all at once.

It would be a while before things got back to the way they were before. Nora was willing to be patient. She'd take one victory at a time.

Nora dashed to her room. After what had happened with Hallie and Lindsay, there was no way she was going to dress up as a pop star. She began sorting through her clothes to see what else she could create.

"Throw a white sheet over your head and be a ghost," Lucas said, sticking his head into her bedroom.

"That's silly," Nora replied. "Everyone knows ghosts don't look like that." She was pulling out paper and colored pens to make a mask. Recalling the drawing he'd left on his bed, she added, "Real ghosts don't go around shouting 'Boo' either."

"Who made you a ghost expert?" Lucas asked as he made himself comfortable on her bed.

"Our building is haunted, you know," Nora told him, as if she'd known it all along and not only just found out. "When I see the ghost on the ninth floor, I'll invite him over for dinner. You can ask him all your questions."

"I'll make a list." Lucas laughed. "So you're going trick-or-treating tonight." He grinned. "Now you really *do* owe me."

"Yes," Nora admitted as she began to draw the outline of a face. "Yes, I do."

CHAPTER 5

Since Caitlin was going to be a zombie, Nora wanted to make a whole new costume in the same category of undead, superscary creatures of the night. She decided to be a vampire.

The mask she created had bloodshot eyes, sharp fangs, and blood dripping down the chin. Nora used a black ribbon to tie it around her head and then put on a black flowing nightgown of her mother's that had been partially burned in the fire. It was what her mother had been wearing when she fought the flames.

The nightgown had charred holes and frayed sleeves. It hung too big on Nora and still smelled like stale smoke. For a vampire costume, it was perfect.

Shoes, however, were a problem. Most of Nora's shoes had been in the living room and turned to ash. They'd never been replaced. She had the tennis shoes she'd worn to the park and a pair of bright pink flip-flops.

Nora looked at her bare feet and wished she wore the same size shoe as her mom. The bedrooms hadn't suffered as much damage as the living room and kitchen. If only Nora had kept her shoes in her room like she'd been told.

Oh well.

What shoes did vampires wear, anyway?

She decided on the flip-flops, hoping that Caitlin might have something better she could borrow. Then Nora checked the time, grabbed an empty pillowcase for candy, and left her apartment. Her ten o'clock curfew was a bummer, but at least she would be out for a while.

As the elevator passed the ninth floor, Nora cupped her ear and listened to the whir of the electric motor. In the apartment building hallway, she could hear a few kids beginning their rounds, knocking on doors and shouting, "Trick or treat," but nothing to indicate a real ghost was roaming around. Not even a clank of chain or muffled, haunted moan.

Disappointed not to have seen a spirit float into the elevator on her way, Nora arrived at the second floor and knocked on Caitlin's door.

The door opened and before Nora had a chance to say hello, Caitlin grabbed her hand and dragged her inside. "Hey, Nora!"

"How'd you recognize me?" Nora asked with a chuckle.

Caitlin pointed down at Nora's shoes. "Fancy footwear for the undead." She laughed.

Nora slipped off her mask. "They were all I could find. I was hoping you might lend me something more vampirey?"

"I have just the thing." Caitlin led Nora to her bedroom. The apartment had the same floor plan as Nora's, but Caitlin lived in Lucas's room, and Nora's room had been decorated as a TV room with large flat screen on one wall, a fancy stereo system, and comfy-looking couches. Nora bet Caitlin had never been poked in the thigh by a broken couch spring.

The hallway was nice, and freshly painted. Family photos hung on the walls. When they reached Caitlin's room, Nora was shocked. It was a mess. Messier than

Lucas's room had ever been. Messier than their whole apartment had been after the firefighters broke down the door and soaked everything with water. Nora had never seen such a disaster.

Clothes were spread on the bed and on the floor, and the closet door couldn't close. School papers and books were scattered over the desk. There was a clean-ish pathway through the room, from the bed to the desk to the door.

A black cat had made itself comfortable on a pile of Caitlin's clothing and was snoozing happily. When Nora walked in, the cat shot to attention, arched its back, and hissed, teeth bared.

"Whoa," Nora said, backing away. "You have an attack cat?"

"I wish. An attack cat would be cool. Bitsy has no nerves at all," Caitlin said. "She's a true-to-life scaredy cat." She clapped her hands and the cat scurried into the corner, where it curled up under a few used towels and immediately went back to sleep.

Nora had to move a stack of gymnastics leotards to sit on Caitlin's beanbag chair, while Caitlin crawled under her bed. "I know they're here somewhere," she said. Her legs stuck out into the room as her head disappeared. "I have these cute black lace-up boots I wore last year when I dressed like a witch. They'd be perfect." Caitlin scooted farther under the bed until she vanished entirely.

"Caity!" A red-haired girl wearing glasses entered the room and dodged around an empty laundry hamper. She was petite and thin and dressed up as a witch. Behind her was a mummy. Nora had no clue what the mummy girl really looked like because she was wrapped head to toe in white gauze. Only her eyes and lips peeked through.

"Hi," the witch said. "You must be Nora."

"Hi," Nora responded. She never felt nervous about meeting new people, but the costumes threw her off a bit.

"I'm Lilly Loughlin. Everyone calls me LL." The witch pointed to the mummy. "That's Aleah."

"Everyone calls me Aleah," the mummy said totally deadpan. Nora giggled and the mummy giggled back.

"Where's Caity?" LL asked.

"Under there." Nora tipped her head toward the bed.

"Figures." LL shook her head. "I worry that she

might get lost in here and never find her way to the door." She waved her hand around the room. "I mean, if anyone ever puts something down and blocks the pathway, Caitlin won't know which way to go."

Nora laughed. She liked Caitlin's friends already.

"I call here every night after practice to make sure Caity made it from the door to the bed," LL said.

"I should write a Halloween story about a girl who gets buried alive, trapped under the weight of her own dirty clothes. That would be scaaarrrryyyy." Aleah chuckled. She explained that she did gymnastics because her parents wanted her to exercise. Aleah's real love was writing stories. She wanted to be a novelist, or maybe a journalist. Or maybe both at the same time. "Do you like being scared?" Aleah asked Nora.

"Love it!" Nora said. "You?"

"Horror stories are my specialty," Aleah said.

"Ridiculous." LL put her hands on her hips. "I don't believe in ghosts or zombies or aliens or any of that. My mom is a scientist and she taught me only to believe in what can be proven." She added, "I'm going to be a scientist too. Gymnastics is just for fun."

"Did Caitlin tell you about the ninth floor?" Nora

asked LL. Scaring someone who didn't believe was the best kind of scaring.

"What about it?" LL asked.

"Shoes!" Caitlin thrust her arm out from under the bed. She was holding two long black boots. Nora reached down to take them. Caitlin was right. They were perfectly vampirey.

Caitlin slithered to the center of the room.

"When I write my story," Aleah told Caitlin, "you'll be trapped under the bed forever, never to return. Ha-ha-ha-ha." She cackled like a witch.

"Hey, that's my laugh," LL said, adjusting her black pointy hat and giving Aleah a small shove. Aleah's legs were wrapped together, so she tumbled back onto the bed, asking, "What sound do mummies make, then?"

"Uh, uh?" Nora suggested.

"That's a zombie," Caitlin said. She stood up and shoved out her hands in a dead walk. She had a fresh layer of under-bed dust covering her already mud-crusted zombie outfit. "Uhhh. Uhhh." Lowering her arms back to her sides, she said, "See? I think the mummy goes, 'Oooooh, oooohhh.'"

"Oooh?" Aleah replied. "That's definitely a ghost."

"No way." Nora was reminded of her conversation with Lucas. "I've never heard a ghost sound like that."

"You've never heard a ghost say anything at all," LL put in. "Because they don't exist."

"Oh yes they do!" Caitlin went to her closet to get the last pieces of her zombie costume. "The ninth floor of this building is totally haunted!"

While Caitlin slipped on a ratty jacket that looked like her father had run over it with the car, Aleah went to the desk and searched for a pen and paper. When she was ready, Aleah told Caitlin, "Tell us what you know and I'll write it up."

"I don't know much," Caitlin admitted.

"Because there isn't anything to know," LL tossed out.

"Spoilsport! Don't ruin the fun!" Aleah turned away from LL and asked Caitlin to give every possible detail. "Go on."

"Okay. I overheard my parents talking the other night. They recently met the people who live in 9G," she began. Caitlin didn't move her clothing off the bed, just sat on top of a pile. "They've lived here for a few years and love the building, but lately some strange things have been happening."

She paused to let the spookiness of the moment sink in. "They hear things through the walls."

"What kind of things?" Nora said. She could feel the hairs on her arms standing on end.

"Pounding, scraping, and squeaking," Caitlin said, wrapping her arms around herself and shivering.

"Ghosts?" Aleah asked.

"It's mice." LL was certain.

"They'd have to be huge mice to make these kinds of noises," Caitlin said.

"Okay, then rats," LL corrected the analysis. "There are extra-big rats in the city. I saw pictures once in one of my mom's *Science Monthly* magazines."

"Eww." Nora would totally rather see a ghost than a rat.

"It's time for trick-or-treating," Caitlin interjected into the conversation.

Aleah said, "There's only one way to know if there's a ghost on the ninth floor or not."

Nora slipped on her mask and picked up her empty pillowcase.

Aleah suggested, "While we are out, we should check out Caitlin's story. They said they heard the sounds through the walls?" She held up the notebook and pen, as if she were a detective ready to investigate a mystery.

"Yes," Caitlin agreed.

Nora laced up Caitlin's boots. They fit.

"We should start on the tenth floor, then," Aleah said. "In the apartment above 9G. Maybe the ghostly noises are coming through the ceiling."

"Uh, Aleah?" Nora knew who lived in 10G. "Hate to be a downer, but Mrs. Daugherty lives in 10G. She's alive. And lives alone. The noises can't possibly be coming from her apartment."

As far as Nora knew, Mrs. Daugherty never talked on the phone. She didn't have kids. No one came to visit. Nora's parents had often said that Mrs. Daugherty was a good neighbor because she never played her TV or radio loudly. Mrs. Daugherty was very quiet.

"We need to snoop around to be sure," Aleah said. She opened the notebook to a blank page and announced, "We're going on a ghost hunt."

CHAPTER 6

"Do your parents let you leave your room like that?" Nora asked Caitlin as they went out into the hallway.

"Caitlin's room is the scariest thing you're going to see this Halloween," LL remarked. "It's totally frightening!"

Caitlin laughed. "They gave up a long time ago." She shrugged. "When we moved in to this new apartment, I tried to keep it clean, but that lasted about a week. I'm barely ever home. Between gymnastics and school and homework, I don't have time to clean it. They told me they'd rather I get good grades than spend my time folding and straightening."

Aleah said, "After I heard about Caitlin's deal, I tried the same argument with my parents. Instead of giving me a pass, they sent me to my room with a dust cloth and a broom."

LL shook her head. "My mom would kill me if I didn't use my drawers or closet."

"Mine too," Nora agreed. Plus, she'd learned the hard way about leaving her stuff lying around in the living room.

The elevator dinged and the four girls got inside. Aleah pressed the button for the tenth floor. The girls chatted about their favorite candies while the elevator moved slowly upward.

As they passed the ninth floor, a rattling sound echoed through the elevator shaft. It didn't sound like a normal elevator sound, more like chains hitting iron.

"What was that?" Aleah looked at Caitlin. "Did you hear that noise?"

"Rats," LL said assuredly, with a *told you so* expression.

"No way," Caitlin said. The noise sounded again. It went *creak-creak-chug-chug-clank-clank*, pause. Then it started again in the same pattern. "That is no rat."

"Yes it is," LL said, though Nora could see she was not as certain as when she'd first identified the sound.

"It's a ghost," Caitlin said in a whisper.

"Or ghosts," Aleah corrected.

LL sighed and shook her head. The sounds had stopped. "R-A-T-S," she said, pointing at the page in Aleah's hand. "Write that down."

Aleah rolled her eyes. "Don't ruin the fun, LL. The ghosts know when there are doubters. They won't show themselves because of your negative energy."

"Negative energy? Don't get me started," LL huffed as the elevator came to a stop.

LL and Aleah ended their argument when Caitlin asked, "Do you want to trick-or-treat at your apartment, Nora?" She glanced up and down the hallway at the different numbers on the doors. "Which one is yours?"

Nora didn't say which and she definitely didn't want to knock on her apartment door. It was still such a disaster inside. Plus she wanted a night away from her family. She simply told them the truth. "My parents never buy candy. My mom's a health freak." She explained that in the past, her mother insisted they hand out something with fewer calories and more nutrition, like carrots. Her dad was the one who let them eat junk on Halloween, but only on that night. The next day whatever Nora brought home (that she didn't hide in her jacket pockets) would be rationed one piece at a time.

In fact, Nora should probably bring a few pieces of whatever she got tonight to Lucas. That would be nice. And she did owe him.

"No offense, but we don't want carrots," Aleah said.

"I don't want them either," Nora replied, sticking out her tongue and gagging. "Although my mom insists they fit the night because they *are* orange."

"Let's start at Mrs. Daugherty's apartment," Caitlin suggested. "If she doesn't answer, we'll know that she died years ago and no one noticed. We can say hi to her ghost."

LL snorted.

"Hmmm." Nora considered that it might be possible. Mrs. Daugherty could have died. Nora hadn't seen the old lady and her pink bathrobe since that night she was interviewed by the TV reporter outside Nora's bedroom window.

They gathered around the doorbell at 10G.

"Who wants to ring?" Caitlin asked. "It's good luck to do the first ring on Halloween."

"You're making that up," LL said. "No such thing as luck. Not good or bad—"

"I'll do it," Nora cut in. To convince her parents to let this be her first outing, not her last, Nora was going to need some good luck.

She rang the bell.

"Who is it?" the old lady asked from inside the apartment.

"Trick or treat," the girls sang out together.

"Oh." Mrs. Daugherty pretended to be surprised to find them all at the door. She opened slowly and peeked through the crack before swinging the door all the way open.

"Let's see here. What do we have this year?" Mrs. Daugherty was wearing a floral dress with the same pink slippers she'd worn on the night of the fire. She glanced around at the four girls. "A zombie." Leaning forward, Mrs. Daugherty put a silver-wrapped piece of chocolate in Caitlin's bag.

"A witch." She gave licorice to LL.

"A mummy."

Aleah got a gumball.

"And"—she looked at Nora's mask—"what are you dressed as, young lady?"

Nora thought it was obvious. "A vampire, Mrs. Daugherty," she replied politely. In a Transylvanian accent, Nora added, "I've come to drink your blood."

"Ha-ha," the old lady chuckled. "So you know my name?" Mrs. Daugherty took a closer look at Nora. "Who is behind that mask? Is it Susie from 4B?"

"Nope." Nora shook her head at the old lady's little game.

"Or Paulina from 6E?"

Nora shook her head again.

Mrs. Daugherty sized her up. "Let me see. You look to be about eleven years old?"

"Twelve." Nora corrected, giving her a hint.

"I don't know." Mrs. Daugherty rubbed her forehead. "Who could it be under the vampire mask?" She shook her head and said, "I give up."

Nora laughed. "Mrs. Daugherty, it's me! Nora Wilson!" She raised the mask so Mrs. Daugherty could see her face.

"AHH!" Mrs. Daugherty screamed. "Ahhh! Ahhh! Ahhh!" She was stuck like a broken record, repeating the same shrieking sound over and over.

"Are you all right?" Nora was concerned. She reached out to touch Mrs. Daugherty's hand. It looked like the woman might be having a stroke. Or a heart attack. Or a seizure.

"No!" Mrs. Daugherty pulled back so fast she stumbled backward into her apartment. "Go away. Leave me alone." She began muttering. "Stay away. Don't come again. Be gone." The door slammed.

Caitlin looked at Nora with wide eyes. "That was weird! Let's get out of here."

The girls grabbed their candy bags and rushed to the elevator.

Mrs. Daugherty's door was closed, but her insane ramblings followed them through the hallway.

LL stabbed the button with her finger, trying to get the elevator to come faster.

Mrs. Daugherty cracked open her door and peeked out into the hall, rubbing her eyes. "It can't be," she mumbled. "Impossible." She blinked a few times, and then began to scream again.

The elevator wasn't coming fast enough. The girls decided to take the stairs.

With Caitlin in the lead they ran, leaping two steps at a time until they reached the ninth-floor landing. Only then did they stop to catch their breath and talk about what happened.

"I don't get it," Nora said. She had goose bumps

down her spine. "Mrs. Daugherty has always been so nice to me."

"That was crazy," Aleah agreed.

"Totally bizarre." Caitlin leaned back against the wall.

"She's bonkers!" LL had no doubt. "That woman needs to see a shrink." She added, "Don't eat her candy. I bet it's poisoned."

They all dumped the one piece out of their bags. Except Nora. Mrs. Daugherty never gave her any candy.

"Well, one thing's for sure," Aleah said, making a note on her paper. "The old woman in 10G is definitely alive."

CHAPTER 7

They opened the stairway door and headed on to the ninth floor. Caitlin led the way and Nora brought up the rear. She was out of breath from running down the stairs . . . and from the fright that Mrs. Daugherty had given them.

"The Hall of Haunts," Aleah said. She had her pen ready to take notes about anything they saw or heard. "How do we get a ghost to show itself?"

"We should just get to the trick-or-treating," LL said. "Look how bad the ghost hunt turned out for us upstairs."

Nora grimaced. "I had no idea I lived next to such a weirdo. She always seemed so nice."

"Ahhh. Ahhh. Ahhh." Caitlin imitated Mrs. Daugherty's shrieks.

"Very funny, Caity." Aleah laughed. "Now, about conjuring these ghosts."

"I know how to do it," Nora said. She remembered a movie she'd watched with her ex-friends. "We need a Ouija board."

"I had one of those once," LL said, surprising everyone. "It's a game board covered with letters. You touch this pointer thing lightly and the ghost is supposed to move the arrow to spell words."

"Did you ever use it?" Aleah asked, her pen poised to take notes.

LL nodded. "A few times, but nothing ever made sense. I thought the ghost was a terrible speller. Then my mom came in and showed me how I was actually moving the pointer myself. Turned out I was the terrible speller."

"Nora, Caity, either of you have a Ouija board?" Aleah asked.

Neither of them did.

"Next idea?" Aleah asked, crossing off the Ouija board from her list.

"I heard that you can conjure ghosts by simply leaving your shoes on the floor. If you want them to stay, line up the shoes neatly, but if you point the toes in different directions, they'll get confused and won't ever come back to that same room," Caitlin said.

"Any ghosts in your bedroom must be super confused," LL said.

"Now you know my secret," Caitlin joked. "That's why there are *no* ghosts in my room."

"That's absurd." Nora laughed. "Any ghost who needs to borrow shoes would probably come to your room first. All that stuff all over the place . . . it's the perfect haunt for the fashionable deceased."

"Glamorous ghosts," Caitlin said with a smile. "They are welcome in my room anytime." She called an invitation into the hallway. "After trick-or-treating, we will be downstairs in 2H. Come visit us."

"I got it! I saw another movie," Nora said, then corrected herself. "Actually, I've seen every ghost movie ever. I think we should try a séance."

"Good idea," Caitlin said as a group of little boys dressed as ninjas knocked on a door nearby and ran off with their bags full of chocolates. She waited until the kids moved down the hallway, then suggested they do the séance around a dark and quiet corner.

"We need to hold hands," Caitlin said. They were

standing in front of an apartment door, but the hall light had burned out. It was hard to see down the dim corridor.

At first LL refused to join the circle. Aleah convinced her by saying, "This is a scientific experiment to see if it's possible to call ghosts."

"Okay, as long as it's science," LL said, taking hands with Nora on one side and Caitlin on the other.

"Talk nicely to them," Nora told Caitlin once they were all connected.

"Of course," Caitlin replied. "I'm always nice." She dropped her voice to a husky whisper, then said, "Oh, mighty ghosts of the ninth floor, we come in peace."

LL rolled her eyes.

Caitlin went on. "We want to be friends. Show yourselves."

The girls all looked around the hallway.

When nothing happened, Caitlin tried again. "Reveal your kindly spectral spheres of light."

"Kindly what?" Aleah interrupted.

"I was giving ghostly compliments," Caitlin explained. "Nora said I should be nice. I was planning to use 'radiant ecto-mist' for a pretty ghost, and for the very intellectual ghost, 'haze of genius.'"

"This is ridiculous." LL dropped hands and broke the circle. "Experiment over," she said. "No more ghosts. It's candy time."

"Come on, LL. Just one more minute," Nora said. She only had another couple of hours to hang out and they still had empty candy bags, but she wasn't willing to give up quite yet.

LL gave in. She rejoined hands with Caitlin and Nora.

"Go ahead," Aleah told Caitlin. "Conjure up a ghost."

Caitlin pressed her lips together, obviously taking the time to plan what she was going to say. "Ninth-floor ghosts," she began. "Hey there, Happy Halloween."

Nora nodded. It was a good beginning.

"We ask that you show yourselves on this special night." Caitlin paused. It was very quiet in the hallway.

"Give us a sign." As she said that, the lightbulb that the girls had thought was burned out flickered on, then went dark again.

LL squeezed Nora's hand. "Probably just coincidence," she whispered. "Electric surge."

"Can you get the ghost to do it again?" Aleah asked Caitlin.

"I don't know." Caitlin stared at the light fixture. She

said loudly into the hallway, "Um, hate to be greedy, but would you mind giving us another sign?" With a glance at Nora, Caitlin added, "Please."

The light flickered the same as before.

"Might be a storm." LL began to pull her hand out of Nora's but Nora held firm. "Anyone see the news? Was rain predicted for tonight?"

Caitlin was honest with the ghost. "Not to be insulting, but my friend doesn't believe in you." She tipped her head toward LL. "Would you mind doing something else? Something different?"

Behind LL's back, the doorknob to the apartment rattled. LL jumped so high, she nearly bumped her head on the light fixture.

"The ghost is trying to get out of the apartment," Aleah said, pointing to the doorknob. It was shaking wildly!

The girls all dropped hands and began to back away from the door.

"Do you need help?" Caitlin asked the ghost. "Are you trapped?"

Clangs came from behind the door.

"Chains," Aleah said. "Ghosts always shake chains."

"It sounded like a spoon hitting a pan," LL said, tilting her ear toward the door.

Nora thought that LL was right, but that didn't make it any less scary when the clangs happened again.

Suddenly, smoke came from under the apartment door. White and thick, it filled the hallway. The chains' rattle became constant. The lightbulb went on and off, flashing like lightning. And the door creaked against its hinges as the doorknob twisted and turned.

"Maybe a séance wasn't such a good idea after all," Nora admitted.

"It might still be a nice friendly ghost like Casper," Caitlin was saying, when the apartment door flew open with a bang and clatter.

"Or a brain-melting poltergeist," Aleah muttered on a sharp inhale of breath.

There in the dim light, shrouded by the fog, was a short figure in a wispy white cloak. The girls froze as the ghostly apparition took a step forward into the hall and said in a raspy voice, "Boo!"

LL, Aleah, Caitlin, and Nora didn't wait around to find out if this ghost was friendly or not.

They ran, screaming just like Mrs. Daugherty.

CHAPTER 8

Back at Caitlin's the girls took off their costumes. They hung out in the TV room and sorted through their treats.

Without all that gauze around Aleah's head, Nora could now see that she was Vietnamese. Her dark hair was cut into a cute bob. Her bangs were mashed flat from being wrapped up for so long. Her brown eyes sparkled as they talked about what had happened earlier on the ninth floor.

The ninth-floor "ghost" turned out to be the old man who lived in the apartment near where they'd had the séance. He played pranks on kids every Halloween. Since Nora had never trick-or-treated in her own building, she hadn't known. When they went running, screaming, down the hall, they'd run into other kids who had fallen for the joke the year before.

LL continued to insist she'd known it was a joke all along.

"You screamed the loudest," Caitlin reminded her.

"It was because he jumped out at us, not because he shouted 'Boo!'" LL told Caitlin. "I was just surprised, not scared."

"If I ever make a haunted house, I'll come up with something scarier to say than 'Boo,'" Nora said as she sat back on what must have been the most comfortable couch in the history of all couches. She put a few of Lucas's favorite candies aside and opened a square of taffy for herself.

"What would you say?" LL asked. "'Oooooh?' And rattle some chains?"

"'Gotcha!'" Nora suggested.

Aleah wrinkled her nose. "How about 'AHHH!'"

"That sounds like the ghost is scared of me, not the other way around," Nora said.

"Well, since there is no such thing as ghosts, I don't think it matters what the ghost says," LL said firmly.

"'Boo' is the best," Caitlin said at last. "Dogs go 'ruff.' Cats 'meow.' Ghosts say 'Boo.' That's how the world works."

"I guess," Nora said as she, Caitlin, and LL started trading candy.

Once everyone had a pile of favorite snacks, Aleah pulled out the laptop she'd brought with her sleepover stuff and logged on to Caitlin's Internet.

"What's the address here?" she asked Nora while her fingers flew over the keyboard.

"One-one-four-four Third Avenue," Nora replied. "What are you doing?" With the sticky taffy in her mouth, it sounded like "Wawa fofo whar yadoin?"

Aleah kept her eyes down. "I'm looking up the history of the building to see if we can track down the ninth-floor ghosts. Maybe if we know how they died, we can do a better job contacting them."

"Great idea!" Caitlin rushed over to where Aleah sat on the TV room floor. She sat cross-legged slightly behind Aleah so that she could see the screen. Caitlin and Aleah both ignored LL when she reminded them that there were no ninth-floor ghosts.

"What's that?" Caitlin asked.

"There was an unsolved disappearance in apartment building 4411," Aleah said. "Not yours."

"Oh." Caitlin was disappointed. "How about that one?" She pointed at another website link.

Aleah let the page load. "Hmmm. There was a severed finger found in the sandbox at the playground across the street."

"Gross!" LL said, holding up her candy sack. "Don't ruin my appetite." Earlier, LL had explained that like Nora's parents, hers would take away whatever candy she brought home. LL's goal was to eat everything in her bag before sunrise.

"So we're looking for a nine-fingered spirit?" Caitlin said. She called out into the room. "Welcome, nine-fingered ghost from the ninth floor. . . ."

"Forget it," Aleah said, scanning the rest of the site. "The finger was plastic. A prank."

"Whew," LL said, stuffing candy corn into her mouth.

"A deadly carbon monoxide gas leak was reported a few months ago in the neighborhood news," Aleah said, then shook her head. "Last week, an elderly man died of natural causes, but he was already in the hospital."

"Seems like the grim reaper has been busy," Nora

commented while she stretched out on the couch and closed her eyes. She knew she had to go home soon, but she was tired. The couch was so comfy.

"Most of the buildings in this area were built in the 1930s. Generations of people have passed through these halls," Nora explained.

"I can't find anything that would help us identify the ninth-floor ghosts," Aleah said. "Let me try a different search. Instead of looking for stories about people who died, I'm going to look up ghost sightings in the area."

"Find anything?" Caitlin asked after a few quiet minutes.

"Two blocks over," Aleah reported, "there was a spectral sighting in an Italian restaurant."

"If you're going to tell ghost stories," LL challenged, "try to scare me. That means you're going to have to do better than haunted meatballs."

"I'm on it." The keyboard clicked under Aleah's fingernails. "How about a disembodied clown that appears at kids' birthday parties?"

"Clowns are scary," Caitlin agreed. "So are floating heads."

"True." LL checked her arms. "But I don't have goose bumps."

"Plus, that sounds pretty far-fetched," said Nora sleepily. "Let's hear a real ghost story."

"Hang on!" Aleah said as she scrolled the cursor around the page. "Here's something really frightening. It's a neighborhood legend. And it is said to have happened only a block away from here."

"Tell us," Caitlin said, stretching her legs out.

Aleah scanned the facts, then told the story in her own way. "A woman met a traveler on the street. He was carrying a worn duffel bag and wearing a tattered army uniform. The man asked the woman for directions. She couldn't hear exactly what he said. He was speaking so softly. She moved closer, and that's when she felt the cold. It was like an icy wind that swept off his skin. She wrapped her light sweater around herself as he spoke again—"

A scratching noise came from inside the wall behind Nora's head.

"Huh?!" Nora sat up. She wasn't tired anymore. "Was that one of you?" She scanned from LL to Aleah to Caitlin.

"No," Caitlin said. Then, "Shhhh." There was the unmistakable clink of chains rattling.

"It's the giant rats," LL said, walking over to the wall. She pounded a fist against a built-in cabinet door. "Back to the sewers!" Then LL turned to Aleah. "You're a good gymnast, but an even better storyteller. I'm not scared, but this one has potential." She gave a fake shiver.

Aleah went on. "'I am lost, ma'am,' he said with a strong foreign accent. His accent was thick, and though the woman was well-traveled, she couldn't figure out where he might be from. 'Can you show me—'"

The scratching noise behind the wall grew louder.

There was a bang and a scrape followed by a rattle.

"It's the ninth-floor ghosts," Caitlin said with certainty. She faced LL. "See that panel on the wall?" She indicated a large square cabinet door set into the wall where the noise was coming from. "My mom told me it used to be an old dumbwaiter. Like a mini elevator used to cart up supplies from the basement back in the olden days. She said it was sealed."

The panel began to shake.

"There's something—*no, someone*—in the dumbwaiter!" Aleah pushed back her computer and grabbed Caitlin around the waist.

The door rattled more as whatever it was in the wall

tried to get out. The painted-over edges of the panel began to peel away. Whatever was back there grunted as the wood began to crack with the force from behind.

"No way," LL muttered in a whisper. "Not scientifically possible." She tilted her head when the next creaks began to ripple through the walls.

"Yes, yes, yes!" Caitlin said, breaking away from Aleah and excitedly rushing to the panel. She was the only one to step forward. Everyone else moved back. Caitlin dragged the couch away from the wall to get closer to the wooden square.

"I did it!" Caitlin announced. "I invited the ghosts and they came." She faced the girls in the room and said, "Happy Halloween!"

"Now I have goose bumps," LL said. "Not even scientific curiosity could get me to open that panel!"

"I'll do it," Caitlin said, her voice strong and fearless.

"No!" Nora and Aleah shouted. But Caitlin ignored them.

Nora's heart raced. Her skin felt cold. But she couldn't look away or even blink. Nora was frozen to the spot, watching, waiting, wondering, as Caitlin slowly reached her arm forward.

CHAPTER 9

With a creak and a crack, the panel shook again.

"I can't do it," Caitlin said as she backed away from the panel. "Is it too late to cancel the invite?" She shouted to the wall, "Stay on the ninth floor, ghosts!"

Aleah started packing up her computer. "I think we should get out of here."

"Rats!" LL said, shuddering. "Gotta be rats."

"I'm being silly," Nora said. She liked scaring people and she loved being scared herself. She was going to face the ghost.

Gathering her courage, Nora approached the panel in the wall.

Behind her Nora's new friends had gathered near the

door, so if things turned badly, they'd be the first ones out of the apartment, out of the building, out of trouble. Nora would be sacrificed to the . . . thing.

"Uuggghhh," the ghost roared as the chains clanked loudly behind the wallpaper.

Nora didn't stop to think about what she'd heard, or wait for the ghost to groan again. If she waited, even a second more, she would lose her nerve. She grabbed a loose corner of the large wooden square and yanked the panel open. She was surprised to find it was hinged on one side like a cabinet door. The door swung open.

Caitlin, Aleah, and LL all shrieked as the ghost tumbled out of the wall and crashed with a familiar heavy clump to the wooden floor.

"Friend or foe?" Caitlin asked, her eyes closed.

"Foe," Nora said without hesitation. "Definitely the enemy."

Lucas lay on the floor behind the couch, rolling around and laughing so hard he had to hold his belly.

Nora stared down on her brother and let out a long breath. "What are you doing here?"

"Did I scare you?" he asked, standing up and surveying each girl's face. "I heard screaming, but it was hard to tell through the wall. Did I? Were you?"

"No!" Caitlin and Aleah declared, glancing tentatively at each other.

"Not me," Nora told Lucas.

"How about you?" He turned to LL. "Were you scared? How about when I shook the panel? That was terrifying, right?"

"A little brother! Ugh. I should have known better," LL said. "When I think that I was *almost* sucked into this nonsense." She stood straighter. "My mom would be so disappointed. She's one hundred percent right. There is no such thing as ghosts." LL put her hands on her hips and snarled at Lucas. "Yes," she admitted. "You got me this time, but it won't happen ever again!"

"One out of four's not bad," Lucas said casually.

Nora could tell he knew he'd really scared them all, even her, a little. He had that twinkle in his eye. She'd never say it out loud, but Nora had to admit that it was a great prank.

"How'd you know about the dumbwaiter?" Nora asked.

Her brother had feathery white dust in his hair and black grease stains on his jeans.

"I told you about the building plans," he reminded her.

"The dumbwaiter is in your room, since that's how the butler would get groceries in and send the trash out. Small things would be hauled up and down this elevator shaft." Since Caitlin's apartment was the same floor plan, they were standing in her old butler pantry too.

"Clever." Caitlin stepped to the opening and stuck her head into the shaft. "It's dark in there."

Lucas shrugged. "I've been experimenting since I first found the panel. It's a tiny space, so I don't really need any light. I sit on the open platform and can move myself up and down, floor to floor."

LL started to reason it all out. "The clanking of the chains must be the sound of you raising and lowering yourself. And the scratching and the rattling, that's you too."

Aleah opened her notebook and reviewed all the things the neighbors on the ninth floor had reported about the ghosts. Nora watched as she crossed off all the clues that were now solved by this discovery.

"No ghosts in the building," she declared.

"Oh man," Caitlin said. She'd gone from determined to find ghosts, to scared to see them, to disappointed they didn't exist, all in one night.

"Told you," LL declared.

"That doesn't mean I can't tell stories to scare us all out of sleeping. Don't forget, there's still the legend of the lost army soldier," Aleah said.

"I'm not going to have any trouble falling asleep," LL declared. "But I'd still like to hear the end. It's entertaining."

"Of course," Caitlin said with a wink to Nora.

"Let me see, where was I?" Aleah lifted the lid of her laptop and settled down onto the floor.

Caitlin asked Lucas, "Do you like scary stories? Aleah was telling us a good one!"

"I like all kinds of stories. Can I stay?" he asked Nora.

"Whatever." Nora didn't want her brother crashing the party, but Caitlin and the others didn't seem to mind. Besides, she didn't have time to argue with him. It was nearly ten o'clock, and she wanted to hear the end of Aleah's story. "Sit." She pointed to the couch that was still pulled out from the wall. The dumbwaiter panel was hanging open. "And no talking."

Zipping his lips and tossing the key, Lucas sat down on the sofa. He couldn't help but open his mouth as he sank into the soft cushions, announcing, "This is so comfy!"

"I know," Nora told him. "Now shhhh."

He rezipped his lips and tossed away another pretend key.

Aleah scrolled through the website to find where she'd been. "Here it is," she said. "So, the woman on the street meets a strangely dressed soldier." Aleah quickly reviewed the story so far. "He asks her for directions. The man makes the woman uneasy, but she moves closer to hear his very soft voice. There is something about his eyes that draws her in. They are glossy black, like a cat's in the dark."

Nora felt that rise of anticipation. She leaned forward, eager to be scared, as Aleah continued.

"The man opened the buttons on his jacket and removed a slip of paper from an inside pocket. The paper was yellowed with age. Tattered around the edges. Folded creases had been there a long, long time, and when he laid the page in his hand, the woman could see splattered reddish-brown stains speckled across the looping cursive words."

"Is all this on the website?" LL interrupted.

"Sort of. The way it's written is so matter-of-fact and boring," Aleah said. "I'm fixing it as I go. Upping the fright-o-meter."

"Good job," LL said. "Go on."

"And it's all true?" Lucas asked.

"Says at the top it is. The author claims he's just reporting the facts of the legend," Aleah said.

"Wow." Lucas raised his eyebrows. "What happened next?"

"So." Aleah took a second to read to get the story in her mind. "The man turned the paper toward her and said, 'I'm seeking this address.' She peered at the page. 'You're not lost,' she told him. 'This is where you need to be.' She indicated the numbers on the outside of the nearest building."

Aleah described how the man reached into his other pocket and pulled out another slip of paper. "Newer than the first, this small slip was white and without folds or splatter marks. 'I'm looking for a woman with this name.' He handed the lady the note. She gasped. 'That's my name,' she—"

Caitlin's doorbell rang.

Nora jumped, not because she was scared, but because it was so unexpected.

"Nora?" Caitlin's father called from the hallway. "Your parents are here."

"Oh no!" Nora jumped up. "I forgot to check the time!" She glanced at a clock. "I'm late getting home." Bummer. She didn't want to leave.

"I better go!" Lucas peeled himself off the couch and hurried into the dumbwaiter. The chains immediately began to rattle as he tugged himself up, raising the platform out of sight. "Close the panel behind me," Lucas shouted down through the shaft.

Caitlin shut the panel while Nora went out into the hallway. LL and Aleah pushed the couch into place.

Nora's mother and father were talking to Caitlin's parents. Nora felt a surge of joy. Maybe things were going to change. Maybe they could all be friends!

"You live upstairs?" Caitlin's mom was asking as Nora stepped into view. She explained how they were new to town. "What apartment are you in?"

"Oh, there you are," Nora's father said, as if seeing her for the first time in the hallway, though she'd been standing there a few seconds already. "It's past curfew, young lady."

"Did you have a nice time?" her mother asked.

"Yes." Nora thanked Caitlin's parents.

Caitlin's mother asked her question again. "You were

about to tell us where you lived. What number apartment is it?"

"Do you have your bag of candy?" Mrs. Wilson asked Nora.

"And your mask?" her father asked. Then, seeing Nora's shoes, he wondered, "Where are your flip-flops?"

"I have them." Caitlin appeared in the hallway. She had Nora's flip-flops, and behind her Aleah and LL had Nora's mask and treats.

There was a lot of hugging before Nora left.

"Thanks for inviting me tonight," Nora said. "Sorry about the ghosts." She winked.

"We can try again next year," Caitlin said with a big grin. "Maybe we'll see a luminous disembodied soul next Halloween." She gave Nora one more hug. "Will you come trick-or-treating again?"

"Of course," Nora said. "Nothing will keep me away!"

"And we'll see you soon," Aleah said. "Right?"

"Of course!" Nora said again. Caitlin was only a few floors down, so she could pop by anytime, and as for the others, she was determined to ask her parents about gymnastics lessons.

As they walked out into the hallway and waited

for the elevator, Nora's dad glanced over Nora's shoulder at her mom, then asked, "Ghosts, huh? What about ghosts?"

"Caitlin heard a rumor that our building is haunted," Nora explained. Her mother appeared frightened at the thought, so Nora said, "We checked around. No real ghosts. All we found was an old man pretending to be a ghost." Then Nora told them, "Aleah did discover a really scary story on the Internet. A creepy thing that happened a block away from here." She told them about the strange soldier as they rode the elevator to the tenth floor.

"What happened at the end?" her mother asked when the elevator door opened.

Nora shrugged and sighed. Her parents had picked her up, that's what happened. But she didn't say that. Instead she answered truthfully, "I have no idea."

CHAPTER 10

Nora went to her room immediately. She didn't want to go to sleep. She wasn't tired. It was still Halloween. Nora had never ended the night without pulling a Halloween prank on Hallie and Lindsay. Well, she'd already pulled one on them today and it hadn't turned out as planned. But Halloween wasn't over yet. This year she decided that she'd prank her new friends, LL, Aleah, and Caitlin!

They were all convinced now that the building wasn't haunted. And they all thought Nora had gone to bed.

All she needed to do was to use the dumbwaiter shaft. The panel in Caitlin's TV room was still loose from when Lucas had fallen through. She could push through it, leap out, and scare them. Her parents would never even know she was gone.

Ha! This would be the best Halloween prank ever.

One of Nora's favorite kitten posters was lying, slightly crumpled, on the floor. Just above it was the panel. Nora couldn't believe that in all the years they'd lived in the apartment, she'd had no idea the dumb-waiter was there. When she'd started collecting posters, her dad had put them up for her. He must have covered the old panel and then forgotten it existed.

"Hey." Lucas stuck his head out of the dumbwaiter shaft and slipped into Nora's room. "Your new friends are way better than your old ones. That was fun tonight!" Lucas yawned. He turned back to shut the panel door, when Nora bolted up off her bed.

"It *was* fun!" She agreed that her new friends were awesome. "And the fun isn't over." Nora asked Lucas to show her how to work the ropes and pulleys to raise and lower the small platform.

Lucas flexed an arm muscle. "It's hard to move the dumbwaiter. You have to control your speed going down." He showed her how to put one hand over the other. "And the way up is even tougher." Lucas imitated a pulling motion. "That's why I got here after you. It takes a lot of muscles to pull your weight up."

"I'm strong enough," Nora said, feeling insulted. She was older and bigger and definitely stronger than Lucas.

Plus, she *really* wanted to get back to the sleepover. She wanted to hear the rest of Aleah's story, eat more candy, and hang out till morning. She could ride the dumbwaiter back up early tomorrow morning before her parents noticed she was gone.

"I'll sneak around with you in the morning," Nora promised her brother. "Right now, I'm going to go—"

"Nora? Lucas?" It was their mom.

Lucas shoved the dumbwaiter panel shut as their parents entered Nora's bedroom. Nora grabbed the baby kitten poster, positioned it over the opening, and struggled to make the torn tape bits stick. When she stepped away from the wall, the poster was crooked, but the panel was covered.

Standing near the dresser, Mrs. Wilson shot the two kids a look. She had an expression that indicated she knew they'd been up to something, but she wasn't sure what. Usually that expression was pointed at Lucas, but tonight she kept staring at Nora. Mrs. Wilson studied her silently for a long time.

"Nora. Lucas. Bedtime," Nora's mother said at last. "Be sure to brush your teeth."

"Blech." Lucas moaned as he turned and walked out of Nora's room toward the bathroom.

"We're locking the front door tonight with the top bolt. Now that we know there are rumors the building is haunted," she told Nora, "we want to keep you and Lucas safe from all those ghost hunters roaming the hallways."

"Oh, Mom," Nora said, rolling her eyes. "I didn't know you believed in ghosts."

"It's not the ghosts," Mrs. Wilson said. "It's the curious strangers who are lurking around tonight. Too many strangers."

Ugh. Nora was immediately reminded just how hard it was going to be to get permission to leave the apartment ever again. She'd thought that since she'd had such a great day, and nothing disastrous had happened, they might come around. But no. They were back to their worried, paranoid ways, not wanting her or Lucas to stray too far or anyone to come near the apartment.

Sheesh, they'd survived a fire! No matter what her parents said about lightning strikes, something that awful could never happen twice. No way! Nora was going to have to show them it was safe for her to be out in the world.

After her parents went to bed, Nora waited a few minutes to make sure no one was coming back to check on her. She carelessly ripped her poster off the wall and dropped it on the floor. Climbing into the dumbwaiter shaft, Nora had to tuck her feet under her legs to make her body small enough to fit in the opening. It was cramped inside, and her right foot immediately fell asleep.

Nora reached out and took hold of one of the thick, rough ropes. With a yank on the pulley to loosen the rope, Nora gripped the frayed cord in both her fists. Then, hand-over-hand like Lucas had shown her, very slowly Nora began to lower herself down.

She got past her own floor without a problem, but as she tried to go below the ninth floor, the rope caught and stuck. It was so dark inside the dumbwaiter that she couldn't see a few inches in front of her. Nora stretched her arms high above her head to feel if the cord had somehow wrapped around the pulley. Everything felt as it should be, but it was almost like there was something propping the dumbwaiter up from below, causing it to stop. With no way to check underneath the base, Nora tugged on the cord to lift herself back onto her own floor. She'd get a flashlight from her room before setting out again.

She pulled. And tugged. And shook the chains that held the platform. The platform refused to budge. It wouldn't go up or down. Nora felt her heartbeat quicken. Why wouldn't the dumbwaiter move?!

Her hands began to sweat and her nerves were on fire.

Nora was trapped inside the wall of the apartment building! Her mind started to play tricks on her. She was seeing shadows that weren't possibly there. Without light how could there be shadows? They'd already proven that the ninth floor wasn't haunted. Or had they?

"No ghosts," she found herself repeating out loud, over and over. "No gh—" When the scratching noises began, Nora remembered what LL and science had said was lurking on the ninth floor.

Something scurried above Nora's head.

"Rats!" she screamed. "Rats!"

In a moment of panic Nora pulled so hard on the rope that it came loose through the pulley. She was no longer in control. The dumbwaiter inched past the eighth floor, the seventh, the sixth . . . The rope slid through her hands as the dumbwaiter continued down, picking up speed as it headed—hurtled—toward the bottom of the shaft.

CHAPTER 11

Nora finally managed get a good hold on the rope. She held the cord so tightly her arm nearly pulled from its socket as the rope dragged her up onto her knees. The rope yanked through her hands. She didn't know which floor she was at now, but she thought maybe she was approaching the second . . . and Caitlin's apartment.

"Help!" Nora cried. She'd planned to scare Caitlin, Aleah, and LL, but now she was the one who was scared. Nora called their names and shouted "Help!" so many times that her throat hurt from screaming.

Slam. Slam. Nora pounded her fists against the wall as the dumbwaiter plummeted toward the second floor. She rotated her body and pressed both arms and both legs into the walls of the dumbwaiter shaft while shouting for help and begging the rats to leave her alone, all at the same time.

The force of her body pressed into the walls caused the dumbwaiter to slow. It didn't stop, but it was enough, if only her friends would open the panel. They had to open the panel!

"Caitlin!" Nora called. "Aleah! LL!"

"Nora?!" Her name was shouted in a chorus of three different voices.

The panel in Caitlin's apartment popped open, and Nora tumbled out and hit the floor with a slam.

Behind her the dumbwaiter continued down until it crashed in the basement. The cracking noise of the base of the box against the cement of the floor reminded Nora what would have happened if her friends hadn't opened the panel in time.

Nora leaped up and hugged each of her friends. "Thank you!" She felt so emotional, tears rolled down her cheeks.

"Are you all right?" Caitlin asked, leading Nora to the sofa.

Nora was shaking. She'd never been so frightened.

"Your hands are freezing cold," Aleah said, grabbing her sleeping bag from the floor, where the girls had positioned their beds. LL and Aleah each took a side, and they wrapped Nora in the fluffy blue sack.

"Here, eat this." LL gave Nora some chocolate. "You're so pale, you're practically blue."

Nora let the chocolate melt on her tongue and ate a few of Caitlin's licorice sticks. The sugar, and time, calmed her nerves, and soon she felt better.

"Thanks," Nora told her friends. "You rescued me."

"We were getting ready to look for a movie on TV," Aleah said, "when we heard you shouting inside the walls."

"We were hoping you'd sneak back," Caitlin admitted. "I somehow imagined it would be with less dramatic an entrance, though." She raised an eyebrow.

"I planned to scare you," Nora told them.

"Well," LL said, "you did do that!" She put an arm around Nora. "We're glad you're okay."

"I'm fine," Nora said. She nodded toward the dumb-waiter shaft. "I'm not sure how I'm going to get home. That was my ride."

"We'll figure everything out tomorrow," Caitlin said. "For now, just enjoy the sleepover."

Aleah read aloud a list of classic horror movies that were playing tonight. Nora had seen them all. And she loved them all.

Caitlin ran to her room and dug up a pillow and a sleeping bag. She handed them to Nora.

Nora knew she shouldn't be there. She knew she was supposed to be upstairs. She knew she had no way to sneak back into her room now. She knew her parents would be mad about the dumbwaiter. She knew all that.

Nora also knew she wasn't ready to go home.

Halloween wasn't over.

Not yet.

As Nora settled in to spend the night, she asked Aleah, "What happened at the end of the story?"

"Story?" Aleah paused the movie. "What story?"

"The soldier. The lady," Nora said. "I left before the end."

"Oh," Aleah told Nora, "I was almost finished. The woman went inside and left him standing on the street." She pressed play on the film. The opening music began. "She called a few friends to tell them what had happened. A few days later she died."

"From what?" Nora asked.

"The website didn't say. I offered to write a better ending," Aleah told Nora. "Caitlin and LL turned me down."

"It's supposed to be true," Caitlin said. "If you made up what happened next, it wouldn't be true."

"Just saying, *my* explanation would have been better than *no* explanation." Aleah shrugged and clicked up the volume on the TV.

"Hmmm." Nora tucked Caitlin's pillow behind her head.

Maybe there was no ending simply because no one, except the soldier and the lady, knew the whole story, and they weren't telling.

CHAPTER 12

As midnight crept closer, the girls were full of candy and growing sleepy. Caitlin's cat was snoozing at the edge of Caitlin's sleeping bag. She was curled up in a tight black fuzz ball and breathing deeply.

"One last story, Aleah. Please." Caitlin wanted to hear another true ghost story before they crashed for the night.

The lights were off. They'd gotten bored with the movies. Aleah's computer screen glowed in the darkness. "I'll find one that will give us all bad dreams," Aleah said with a chuckle.

"I'll sleep like a baby," LL assured her. "Don't worry about me."

"Sounds like a challenge," Aleah told LL. Everyone sat quietly while Aleah browsed websites. The only noise was her fingers striking keyboard keys, until she said, "Okay. I think— Wait. What's this?" Aleah leaned forward so that her face was eerily illuminated by the screen. "Here it is. What I'd been looking for all along. A story about this exact building."

"Ha! I knew it!" Caitlin pumped the air. "There is a ghost on the ninth floor after all."

"No." Aleah scanned through the story, then reported, "But I think this might be the source of the ghost rumor, Caitlin." She began to retell the news story. "Earlier tonight, I looked for stories about people who died, or ghost stories. This is different. This is about a fire."

"A fire?" Nora had been lying down on the sleeping bag. Now she sat up and moved to the edge of her bedding. A chill rose up her spine as Aleah began to interpret the report in her own storyteller style.

"The fire began in the kitchen." Aleah's voice was soft and vibrated through the silence. "It was so late at night, it was early in the morning. Very few people in the building were awake."

The way Aleah was speaking drew them all into the

story. LL came and sat next to Nora. Caitlin moved near Aleah. They were in a circle, knees touching.

"Four people lived in the apartment. A mother. A father. And two children."

Nora knew this story. But she didn't say anything, not yet.

"The blaze quickly spread from the kitchen into the living room, turning everything it touched into hot white ash. The mother and father fought the flames with water, blankets, and an old fire extinguisher they'd had in the pantry but had forgotten to replace when it expired."

Nora could smell the smoke on her pajamas. The constant reminder . . .

"The neighbors could hear the children screaming. They reported that the parents sent the kids to safety in a back bedroom. It isn't fire that usually kills in these situations, it's the smoke. They warned the children to stay close to the floor and not to open any windows, for fear of—"

"Backdraft," Nora supplied the word.

Aleah glanced up at her with curiosity. Nora shrugged as if it was a common phrase that everyone should know, and Aleah went on.

"Men and women from the surrounding apartments tried to open the front door, but it was jammed. They wanted to help, but the heat was intense. Smoke was filling the hallway, making it hard for the rescuers to breathe."

"This is horrible!" Caitlin said. "When did it happen?"

Aleah scrolled down the page. "Um, actually, just before your family moved to town."

"What happened next?" LL asked. "I hope the fire department came."

"They did," Nora said, adding, "But the reporter arrived first."

Everyone turned to look at her.

"I forgot you've lived in this apartment building a long time," Caitlin said.

"All my life," Nora replied.

"Were you here the day of the fire?" LL asked. "It sounds so awful."

Nora nodded, small and timid. "I was here."

She'd never talked to anyone except her family about the fire before. Nora could see the other girls were anxious to hear her firsthand account. Not that she didn't want to tell them. It just felt so strange. The fire. What happened after. Her parents' freak-out. The homeschooling and their refusal to let her do anything, because they were intensely afraid of the world.

She just wanted to be Normal Nora.

Not this Nora, the girl who'd survived a fire.

Aleah, always seeking the facts, asked, "Did you know that the fire investigator reported that the fire started because of exposed electrical wiring in—"

"In the oven," Nora finished. "Yes. They said that."

"The fire department told *you*?" Caitlin reached out and put a hand on Nora's knee. It was a sign of trust and friendship.

Nora put her own hand on top of Caitlin's and gave it a squeeze. "They didn't have to tell me."

LL and Aleah reached out and instinctively put their own hands on Nora's and Caitlin's, forming a pile. Nora took a deep breath. "I could hear them talking."

Get it done and tell the truth. Nora blurted out the last bit.

"The firefighters were standing in my kitchen."

CHAPTER 13

"We survived." All eyes were looking at Nora. "We hid in my bedroom while the firefighters broke down the front door."

"Awful!" LL exclaimed. "You must have been so scared."

Nora thought back to that morning. Oddly, she didn't recall feeling fear. Her parents were so mellow about it all. Her dad said they'd be fine, and she believed him. "We could hear the fire trucks outside. And the voices in the hall." Memories flooded over Nora. "I never thought that we might die. Or if I thought it, I never let the idea stick."

No one asked any questions, so Nora went on. "The

worst part was the heat. And the smoke." She shivered. "It was hard to breathe."

"Now I have goose bumps." LL rubbed her arms.

Caitlin put her arm around Nora. "So the fire department broke down the door?"

"Yes," Nora said. She was actually relieved to be telling her new friends about that day. "They used axes to knock it down, then burst in with water hoses." She closed her eyes as she recalled the strong woman who had picked her up and carried her down the apartment stairs. Nora had rested her head against the woman's shoulder. She'd smelled like rose water perfume. It was a million times better than the smoke, and Nora hadn't wanted to be set down when they reached the sidewalk.

"My mom, Dad, me, and Lucas, we were all put in an ambulance and given oxygen." Nora cupped her hand over her mouth to show them what it was like. She could hear them all inhale as if reliving the experience alongside her.

"I should write this down for you," Aleah said. "You might want to write a book someday."

"I don't think I'll ever forget the details of that night," Nora told her, then added, "You can write the book about me, if you want." She considered the project and said, "I might draw the pictures for it." After she took art classes, of course. If gymnastics wasn't a perfect fit, art classes could be next on the list of things to try.

Having spent so much time with Caitlin and her friends that night, Nora was now even more determined to find something she was really, really good at.

"What happened next?" LL asked.

Nora started to spill all about her parents and their financial cutbacks and school, but suddenly stopped herself. "Can I use your computer for a sec?" Nora asked Aleah.

"Sure," Aleah said. She turned the laptop toward Nora.

Nora stared down at the keyboard. How long had it been since her computer had fried in the fire? Two months, but it felt like forever since she'd typed. Nora ran her fingers across the keys. They made little clicky noises. It was all she could do to stay focused on what she wanted to show her friends instead of taking a few minutes extra to check her e-mail account. Though who would e-mail her? Not like Hallie and Lindsay were sending messages.

She'd love to play a game. There were so many she'd liked before her parents let the Internet go.

Nora used to like surfing around websites. Reading strange facts, movie reviews, the latest fashion, watching funny videos. She set her hands flat over Aleah's keyboard and wondered what had happened on all her favorite TV shows.

It was amazing how much she'd taken her computer and the Internet for granted when she'd had them, and how much she missed it now that she didn't.

Nora sighed.

And focused.

She typed information about the fire into the search bar.

Only one video popped up.

"Here." Nora turned the screen so that everyone could see. And then she pressed play.

The blond reporter, the one who had been the first to arrive on the scene, was standing on the sidewalk below Nora's window, holding a microphone in her hand.

Nora sat up straighter. She'd never actually seen the news report. This first part was what she'd seen through her window.

A few minutes in, Mrs. Daugherty came out onto the sidewalk in her pink robe and slippers.

"Isn't that—" LL began.

The others shushed her.

Nora nodded.

"I smelled the smoke in my apartment," the old lady said. "There are children up there." She pointed at Nora's bedroom window. "Help them!"

The camera panned up and Nora wondered if they hadn't done some fancy editing back at the studio. There she was waving. She was certain that she'd waved earlier on. Not while Mrs. Daugherty was being interviewed. While watching the newscast, Nora's brain felt heavy and the details seemed fuzzy.

Things didn't appear to be unfolding as she remembered.

The sirens sounded higher pitched. The smoke pouring from the building was darker gray. She was seeing the event from a whole other perspective. It felt removed, like a movie of someone else's story, not her history.

Nora shook her head as she watched the firefighter carry her to the ambulance. Behind her, so close to Nora she could have reached out and touched his hand, was a soldier. In a strange old-fashioned jacket.

Forgetting for an instant that her friends were also watching, Nora reached forward and paused the video. Something was very odd. The soldier seemed to be whispering something in her ear.

"Do you see that guy?" Nora asked her friends, pointing at the screen. "The one in the old uniform?"

"No," LL said. "Just you and the firefighters. What do you see?"

"I don't know." Nora fell silent as she stared at the man on the screen.

"Press play," Caitlin said. Her voice effectively zapped Nora out of her fog.

She tapped the cursor and stared at the screen as the man disappeared behind a police car.

The next part Nora recalled clearly. Other firefighters brought Lucas, and two others escorted her parents down. They all sat in the ambulance for a short time, breathing through oxygen masks until they were cleared as being healthy.

Then her family stepped into a cheering crowd and faced the reporter's microphone.

The blonde on the computer screen shoved the microphone into Nora's face.

Nora remembered thinking her hair was a mess, there was soot on her face, and she was wearing pajamas. Not exactly the way she wanted to present herself the first time she was on TV.

On-screen, Nora watched as she fidgeted with her hair and tried in vain to cover her pajamas with her arms.

The reporter asked her, "What happened up there?"

Nora began to answer, when Lucas popped his head into the frame. "We had a fire." Then he waved at the camera. "Hello!" he shouted.

The reporter moved away from Nora to ask her parents a few questions. Her father mentioned that he'd reported the faulty oven wiring many times to the property manager, but had never had a response.

The reporter asked, "Do you have rental insurance to cover the damages?"

Her father shook his head solemnly. "No. The fire wasn't our fault. We can't afford to go anywhere else. We'll have to stay here while the apartment is repaired."

That was the beginning. Nora could see the shift, right there, right then, in her father's face.

It was the responsibility of the owner of the building and the property manager to set things straight. Her dad wasn't going to budge, not him or his family, until they fixed the apartment.

"We won't leave." He'd made his threat on live TV.

Nora knew now that the threat hadn't worked.

They hadn't left the apartment, but nothing had been fixed either.

"We don't believe the fire is our responsibility," the owner of the building was now saying in a separate interview. "The wiring was old, but safe. We will be conducting an investigation to find out the real cause of the fire. The tenants will need to pay for the repairs themselves. If they don't cover the costs, when the family goes out—for groceries, dinner, food—we will lock them out."

"We aren't going anywhere," Nora's mother told the reporter.

It was a battle of wills between her parents and the people in charge of the building.

The video faded to black and Nora sighed.

"Wow," Caitlin said as Nora passed the computer back to Aleah. "A fire."

"Yeah," Nora said.

"Your parents are tough," Aleah said.

"I know," Nora replied. Boy, were they!

"You're really lucky to have survived," LL told Nora.

"Yes," Nora agreed. "Very lucky." She had a headache. So much information in that video. And so much she didn't understand.

"You look tired," Aleah noted. "Trick-or-treating, ghost hunting, falling down a pitch-black shaft—a lot has happened tonight!"

Nora nodded.

"Why don't we all go to sleep," Caitlin suggested, slipping away and settling into her sleeping bag. "We can talk more tomorrow."

The others agreed. Nora didn't say anything. She felt a thousand emotions: sad that she'd missed so much of the world outside her apartment, mad at her parents' stubbornness, frustrated that she was caught in the middle of their feud with the landlord, sympathetic to their determination to see things set right.

She was confused and tired. So very tired.

But as she closed her eyes, one emotion felt bigger than all the others.

It was happiness.

With all that had happened, Nora was grateful to be alive.

CHAPTER 14

"Hello, Nora," the man said in a voice so soft she could barely hear his words. Nora sat up in her sleeping bag. She knew she was dreaming and tried to wake herself up. Pinching her arms didn't help. The girls were all asleep on the floor nearby. None of them saw the man sitting in a chair that didn't exist, or heard him speaking in an indistinguishable accent from some faraway country.

Only her.

Nora wasn't afraid. "I saw you on the video. You were there, at the fire."

"Yes," he said in his strange accent. "I visited you there. Do you remember what I said?"

Nora thought about that day. She replayed the video

in her head. "No," she admitted. "What was the message?"

"I said that it wasn't your time." The man leaned back in the chair.

Nora considered that. "And the woman who disappeared? The one from the Internet story? You were the one who asked her for directions. What about her?"

"Her time had come," he said simply.

This was an odd conversation in a bizarre dream. Nora pinched herself again, thinking it would be best to wake up and get this guy out of her head. No matter how hard she pinched her leg, he wouldn't disappear.

As long as he stayed, she had a question for him. She didn't know why she wanted to know, but she did. "When will it be my time?" Nora let the question hang in the air.

"It already passed," he said before fading into the darkness.

Nora stared at the empty spot where he'd been sitting and shook her head. What did that mean: *It already passed*? It made no sense at all.

He'd never actually mentioned death. Could it be that there was something else he was talking about? Nora was so confused. And the more she thought about his words, the more her confusion grew.

It wasn't possible. It couldn't be . . .

"No! No! No! I don't want to die!"

Nora woke up screaming.

She was awake. That was for certain.

She'd been screaming. That was for certain too.

So why were her friends all still asleep?

"Caitlin?" Nora got out of her sleeping bag and went over to Caitlin. She was the closest.

"Caity?" Nora poked Caitlin on the arm.

"Ugrla," Caitlin mumbled, swatting at Nora as if she was a bug and rolling over before letting out a huge snore.

"Wow. She must be exhausted," Nora said, moving on to wake up LL. She stepped over LL's duffel bag and quietly bent down next to her pillow.

"Hey," she whispered in LL's ear. "I can't sleep. I had a bad dream. Wake up and hang out with me."

LL didn't move. Nora tried to get Aleah to wake up, but same thing. She was crashed out. Nora checked the time. It had only been a few hours since they'd gone to bed. No wonder no one had heard her scream or woke up now. They were all sound asleep.

The first rays of sunlight were starting to turn the sky orange and yellow. Nora sat down on the couch and wondered if the girls would wake up when the room was completely filled with light, or if they'd sleep a lot later than that. She hoped the light would get them up.

To waste time, she flipped through one of Caitlin's gymnastics magazines while she waited.

When the sun was fully round in the sky, Caitlin began to stir.

"Hi." Nora was happy when Caitlin peeled out of her sleeping bag and stood up. She'd been lonely.

"Where's Nora?" Caitlin woke up Aleah.

Aleah yawned. "What do you mean?"

"Yeah," Nora asked Caitlin, "what do you mean? I'm right here."

"Did she go home?" Aleah asked Caitlin.

Caitlin shrugged, and then they both woke LL.

"Go away," LL muttered, slinking down into her sleeping bag like a turtle into a shell. "Studies show that the average person needs six to eight hours of sleep, or else."

"Nora's gone," Aleah said. "Did she tell you she was leaving?"

"No." LL looked at Nora's empty sleeping bag.

"Heeellllooo." Getting off the couch, Nora stepped into the center of the room. She waved her arms and stomped her feet. "I'm right here."

LL looked toward her but didn't make eye contact. Caitlin's cat, however, hissed at Nora.

Ignoring the feline's glare and knowing she was a scaredy-cat, Nora stomped louder. The cat scurried away, but no one else reacted to the noise.

Nora got right up into Caitlin's face. "Can't you see me?" she asked, beginning to wonder if maybe this was part of that odd dream she'd been having. It was possible that Nora was still asleep.

"I thought she had a good time," Caitlin said with a frown. "I don't understand why Nora ditched out."

"Maybe her parents discovered she was missing and came to get her?" Aleah suggested. "They are worriers."

"And she left without saying good-bye?" Caitlin wrinkled her nose. "I don't know Nora very well, but after what she did to get here"—Caitlin pointed to the dumbwaiter panel—"it's hard to believe that she'd leave without a word."

"Maybe she left a note," LL suggested.

"No note," Nora said. "Come on, guys. I didn't leave."

She lay back down on her sleeping bag and closed her eyes. "Okay," Nora told herself. "I know you're tired, but it's time to wake up." She acted like she was hypnotized. "On the count of three, you are going to open your eyes and be awake." She counted. On three, Nora snapped her fingers and opened her eyes.

"Ugh!" Nora rolled out of the bag and onto the floor as Caitlin swept up the bag and Aleah took the pillow out from under her head.

"I'll toss these in my room. Then let's get breakfast," Caitlin told the others. It was as if they'd given up looking for Nora.

"But I'm here," Nora said, her voice dropping as sorrow sank in. "Why can't you see me?"

Nora followed the girls down the hallway into Caitlin's messy room. Caitlin tossed the sleeping bag and pillow onto the beanbag chair and said, "Maybe this afternoon we should go up to the tenth floor and check on her. I bet Aleah's right, her parents must have found out she wasn't in her own bed and come down to get her."

"Makes the most sense," LL said with a nod. "Nora's so nice she probably didn't want to wake us all up."

They all agreed that was what had happened and

that after breakfast they'd go knock on Nora's door.

"But . . ." Nora began to follow them to the kitchen. She was still confused, but now she felt another emotion: anger that they were ignoring her. "Hey!" Nora exclaimed as Caitlin shut her bedroom door. The door slammed hard in Nora's face. It should have hurt, but it didn't.

"That's weird," Nora said with a shiver as she realized the door had passed *through* her. It hadn't actually hit her.

Maybe the girls were playing one last Halloween prank on her? Nora had to get out of there to find out.

As she reached for the knob, Nora noticed there was a mirror on the back of Caitlin's door.

She didn't see herself in the glass. "Huh?" Nora got closer. In Caitlin's messy room it was possible the glass was dirty or . . .

No. The mirror was the cleanest thing in the room.

Nora got so close to the reflective surface that she should have seen the flecks of gold in her eyes. She should have been able to count every freckle on her face. She should have seen—well, she should have seen her reflection.

But Nora didn't appear in the glass.

Nora was invisible.

CHAPTER 15

"You're not invisible," Nora's mother explained after Nora had told her what happened at Caitlin's. "You're a ghost."

"We all are," her father said.

Nora was back in her own apartment, sitting on the smoky, burned, and uncomfortable red velvet sofa.

After discovering she didn't need to open the door to leave Caitlin's bedroom, Nora slid through the apartment door at Caitlin's, took the elevator up, and stormed into her own apartment without turning the knob.

Her parents were upset that she'd snuck out and been gone all night.

"Go ahead and punish me!" Nora exclaimed. "What

are you going to do? *Kill me?* I'm already dead!" So it wasn't the best way to handle the situation, but Nora was furious. "You should have told me!"

"What's going on?" Lucas came in from his bedroom just then. His hair was sticking straight up. "What's with all the shouting?" He rubbed the sleep from his eyes and looked at his sister. "Nora?"

"Ask them," Nora growled.

That was when the Wilsons called a family meeting. The third in Nora's life. No, actually the third since Nora's death.

Lucas sat next to Nora on the couch. Their parents both stood.

"I'm a ghost?" Lucas asked. He was very excited to hear it. "That explains so many things!" He gave a sigh of relief. "I was beginning to think Mom and Dad were crazy," he told Nora. "They aren't crazy! They're dead. We all are!" Lucas bounced on a squeaky couch spring. "This is great news."

Nora spun to face her brother. "What is so great about it?"

"Well," Lucas said, "think of the adventures we can have."

Nora plugged her ears. "No adventures." She rotated back to face her parents. "How did this happen?" Nora needed to know. "I saw the newscast. I *know* we were rescued."

"Oh. Right." Lucas stopped bouncing. "I remember the fireman who carried me downstairs."

The mystery deepened.

Nora's father began the explanation. "Yes, Nora. We were all rescued. But the person who owned the building insisted the fire was our fault and claimed we should pay for the damages."

"I saw the report. You didn't have insurance." Nora wanted him to skip forward to the dead part of the story.

"We couldn't afford to fix the apartment." Mrs. Wilson picked up the telling. "And it *wasn't* our fault." She looked at Lucas since he was the one who hadn't seen the TV newscast. "So, after the fire was out and we could come back to the apartment, we refused to leave. And the person in charge refused to fix the damage."

"A week passed." Mr. Wilson paced the living room as he spoke, and Nora was reminded about the people on the ninth floor who heard ghosts moving around.

The haunting was in 10H. Her apartment.

"Then apartment management cut off our phones and refused to allow anyone up to see us," Nora's mom said. "We were at a stalemate with the apartment owner. No repairs were done. I didn't want you kids to go to school for fear that you couldn't get back inside. I was worried that someone would nab you and use you to lure us out. I was stubborn."

She went on. "And frustrated. It was hard, but I used every argument I could think of to convince your dad that we needed to leave the apartment. We needed to hire a lawyer. I mean, we'd filed maintenance reports and those were public record. The fire department had confirmed that the fire was caused by faulty wiring. There was no way we'd lose a lawsuit. They'd have to fix the apartment."

"I finally agreed." Mr. Wilson stopped pacing. He put an arm around his wife.

"I went to see a lawyer." She glanced at the door. "But couldn't leave."

"What do you mean, 'couldn't'?" Nora asked.

"Was the door jammed like in the fire?" Lucas asked.

"No," Mrs. Wilson replied. "My feet couldn't cross the

doorway downstairs, the one leading outside the building."

"I tried also," Mr. Wilson put in. "It was as if there was an invisible wall."

"That's when we discovered that there had been a carbon monoxide leak," Nora's mom began. "We don't know where the leak came from, but it must have happened while we slept. We never realized that the carbon monoxide detector was destroyed in the fire so the alarm never went off. We'd been dead awhile before we realized what had happened."

Nora remembered Aleah mentioning a carbon monoxide news item when she'd been looking for horror stories online. Nora just hadn't realized that particular story was about her family.

"I didn't know we'd all died until that moment," Mrs. Wilson said, her voice cracking.

"Why didn't you tell us right away?" Nora asked. "We'd have understood."

"Get real." Lucas gave Nora a shove. "We'd never have believed them."

"We wanted to shield you from the news for as long as we could," Mrs. Wilson said. "Plus we didn't know how this ghost stuff works."

"I can walk through walls," Nora reported. "That's how I came home this morning."

"Sooooo coool!" Lucas said. Nora could see his head spinning with a plan to use his newly discovered superpower. "We can fix the dumbwaiter and do all sorts of things."

At Nora's parents' questioning glance, she explained how she'd gone down to Caitlin's in the dumbwaiter. She'd left that part out when she'd stomped into the apartment, demanding answers. They'd asked where she'd been, but hadn't stopped to wonder how she'd gotten there in the first place. The door was still locked, after all, not that it actually mattered.

"Not like I was in any mortal danger," Nora said with half a smile.

Her mother gave Nora a glare. "You left the apartment without permission. You will be punished."

"Ugh." Nora rolled her eyes. "I'm a ghost! Isn't that punishment enough?"

In that moment, Nora realized what she was good at. She didn't need art classes or gymnastics, or dance, or theater, or anything else. Nora was good at Halloween! She was great at scaring people. That was her best and favorite skill, and now she would be scary *forever*. No costume necessary.

Nora had a goal. And it was a doozy.

She smiled. She finally understood what her parents meant when they'd said "the veil was thinner." It meant she could be seen on Halloween. She could even leave the building, but only on that one day.

"I was thinking we don't need to wait until next Halloween to start haunting," Lucas said. "We can begin sneaking around the building today. Let's take stuff off Mrs. Daugherty's tables. Rearrange her furniture. We can hide her slippers in funny places." He clumped his way across the room. "Does it hurt when you pass through?"

"I don't know about the walls. Going through doors didn't hurt," Nora replied. "It was easy."

"Oh yeah!" Lucas fist-pumped the air. "I can't wait to get started."

"Nora, you are grounded for a week. After that, there will be rules," Mrs. Wilson said. She had a very serious look as she shook her head. "We are still having home-school. And you can't go out of our apartment without permission. We need to know where you are. And—"

Interrupting, Mr. Wilson winked at the kids. "I want to come along sometimes."

—————————————————————

As part of their science homework that evening, Nora and Lucas were discussing how they were going to fish the dumbwaiter out of the basement. They'd convinced their mom that it was a physics issue and raising the platform would involve math skills.

Suddenly the knob on the front door turned. Nora and Lucas looked up.

"Did you lock the door when you came in this morning?" Nora's father asked, setting down the book he was reading.

"I walked straight through the wood, remember?" Nora said.

There were voices in the hall.

"I was worried about this," Nora's mother said. "Ghost hunters." She shooed the kids into Nora's room. "They'll come in with their infrared cameras and EMF meters. If they find signs of paranormal activity, we will never be left alone again!"

"We need to convince Mom and Dad that it's our

duty to scare the hunters away." Lucas smiled. "We don't want anyone to move in, so we need to keep up the fright factor."

Standing on Nora's bed, Lucas began to jump up and down. "How cool is this? We need to 'borrow' a Ouija board from a neighbor. We could use it to practice our spelling words for school." Lucas swiveled his hands as if he were working the pointer. "Tonight, I hope someone does a séance. I have some messages I'd like to pass to the living." He flopped back on the mattress with a final body bounce and giggled. "We can make up anything we want."

Nora rolled her eyes. "Or we can scream 'Boo!'" She sat down on the bed near Lucas's feet.

"Yeah," Lucas said dreamily. "That's awesome."

"Shhh," Nora's father warned. "I can see that your mother was right. We need to discuss the parameters of this haunting thing. Until then"—he put a finger over his lips—"no noise."

Whoever was on the other side of the door picked the lock and came in. Nora realized that she recognized the voices entering the apartment.

"Mom, wait!" she said, before her mother shut Nora's

bedroom door and barricaded it. "That's Caitlin." She cupped her ear. "And LL. And Aleah." Nora could hear them comment on the empty apartment. "They're looking for me."

"Get out there and start haunting!" Lucas kicked Nora in the back. She fell off the bed, landing on the floor with a heavy thump.

"What was that?" Caitlin's nervous voice echoed through the burned-out space.

"A big rat?" LL sounded scared as she admitted, "I don't know." Nora liked that she'd finally gotten under LL's skin. The scientist was a little less sure of herself now.

Aleah was definitely scared. "I think we should go downstairs," she said with a quiver. "I don't see Nora anywhere. In fact, it doesn't look like anyone lives here. How could they? This is just a burned-out shell of an apartment."

"Come on, Nora." Lucas sat up on the bed. "Let's give them a real fright."

"I think I already did," Nora said, considering how she'd disappeared from their sleepover, and then when they'd gone to find her, they'd discovered that her apartment was empty. Nora smiled. "I'll let them freak out a little for now. They should wonder what happened to me. Leave a bit of mystery. And then haunt them all year, just a tiny scare at a time."

"Build it up for a big Halloween surprise?" Lucas asked as the front door to the apartment slammed shut.

"For sure!" Nora went out into the living room and stared at the back of the door. She could hear her friends' footsteps, as they decided to take the stairs, too frightened to stay on the tenth floor and wait for the elevator.

Nora smiled. "Next year will be the best Halloween ever."

EPILOGUE

364 DAYS LATER . . .

Nora was hiding behind the couch when she heard the voices. She didn't want to be seen until the moment was right.

Caitlin and Lindsay were following Hallie through the front doorway of Hallie's apartment. LL and Aleah were with them. They were all friends now.

"I think it's great that we all wore matching costumes," Caitlin said, cheerfully pulling off her wig. Her bracelets jangled as she brought her arm back down.

"We were the most awesome hippies out there," Aleah replied in a far-out voice.

"Totally, yeah," said LL, giving the peace symbol.

"Now let's check out our loot." She dumped her candy onto Hallie's family room floor. The girls had set out sleeping bags for a slumber party.

Nora knew they were planning to watch scary movies. She was going to make the night even scarier.

Looking over her collection of candy bars and other wrapped snacks, Lindsay said, "Our apartment building has the best trick-or-treating." She raised a handful of treats and let them rain through her fingers. "So much candy."

"Last year LL and I had a good time at Caitlin's," Aleah said, as if she'd forgotten that Nora had gone with them. Or tried to forget. "But this year was totally better. Way more candy."

Nora would have to make sure that no one forgot her after this year.

"Ready?" Lucas whispered, settling down into the small hiding space beside her. He was wearing a white sheet with holes cut out for the eyes. Classic ghost.

Her brother was as annoying as ever, but now instead of chasing him away, Nora hung out with him. They were partners in haunting, and business was booming.

Turned out they didn't need to fix the dumbwaiter in

their building at all. With a little practice, they discovered they could go up and down all they wanted by melting through doors, walls, and even ceilings. Haunting inside the apartment building was great, but tonight was Halloween. Time to up the scares a lot. Maximum fright.

"Do you have the supplies?" Nora asked her brother.

He held up a canvas sack. Over the year, he and Nora had collected the perfect haunting supplies. They'd all been tested, effectively convincing the family in 6C to move away.

Haunting their own building was fun, but Nora had been waiting for this night for fifty-two weeks—364 long days and nights.

LL and Aleah climbed into sleeping bags while Caitlin and Hallie set up the first movie. Lindsay turned down the lights.

The TV cast an eerie glow across the room and set the perfect mood for haunting.

Nora gave Lucas a nod. He laid out his supplies behind the couch.

Lucas was not only an excellent actor, but he was a great director, too. They'd prepared a perfectly staged production.

Their show started with a bell. Lucas rang it near the TV once, then moved to the other side of the room. He moved around, in and out of walls so no one could see him, not yet. It was something Nora and Lucas had just discovered that night. On Halloween they could be seen, but only if they wanted to be seen.

The girls sat up on their beds, looking around for the source of the chimes, but never saw anything. Lucas came back to the couch and handed the bell to Nora. Then he went around the apartment stomping his feet and slamming doors.

He crashed and clomped until Lindsay got up and turned the light back on.

"That's odd," she said with a shiver. "So much noise."

"The people upstairs must be having a party," LL remarked.

Nora winked at Lucas. It was time for phase three. He rattled chains. At the same time, Nora moved to the switch and turned the lights all off again.

Lindsay turned them on.

Nora turned them off.

It was a game for Nora and her brother. For Lindsay and the others, it wasn't very fun. Their faces were growing pale. Their eyes began to bulge. Nora could see a bead of sweat on Hallie's forehead and goose bumps on LL's arms.

Next came the howling. Nora loved this part. "Oooohhhh," she moaned. "Oooohhhhh."

Through their experimental haunts over the past year, Nora had discovered that people were most scared when the ghosts did exactly what they expected them to do. Rattle chains. Slam doors. Move stuff around like a poltergeist might. If the ghost did something unexpected, it was easier to say it was a trick of the mind or a play of the imagination. Predictable ghosts were the terrifying kind.

While it was dark, Nora took a flashlight from the bag and shone it on Lucas and his sheet. He seemed to glow as he stepped through a wall like an actor coming onto the stage. This was the best part. Playing a ghostly visitor, he dramatically set a Ouija board down on the floor. Lucas carefully placed the pointer in the center, in the middle of all the letters.

Lindsay and Hallie huddled together in a corner, watching the sheet move across the room. "This is scarier than any movie," Hallie squeaked, her voice shaky and barely audible.

LL stared at the board with her mouth hanging open. Aleah held her hand. "What do we do?" she breathed.

"I think the ghost wants to talk to us," Caitlin said. Nora could see her swallow hard as she moved to the board.

Caitlin lightly touched the pointer. Nora slipped behind her to guide her hand in the darkness. Lucas shone the flashlight on the board.

"N." Caitlin reported the first letter.

"O." The second one.

"Could it be?" Aleah said with a shudder.

"R." There was only one more letter to go.

"A."

Silence. The girls were all too scared to speak. It would be nice if they said *Hello*, Nora thought, but she knew that wasn't going to happen. She was a ghost, after all. And ghosts were scary, right? No sense in saying hi to a ghost.

Caitlin sat still, her fingers hovering over the last letter in Nora's name, waiting to see if there was more.

There was. But not another letter. Not what any of them expected.

On a silent count of three, Lucas flicked on the lights.

Nora slipped under the floorboards and popped up from beneath, up through the Ouija board.

"Boo!" she shouted, because that's what ghosts said.

The screaming went on for a long, long time.

"Good work tonight." Lucas gave Nora a high five as they walked home together.

"That was fun," Nora said. "I can't wait for next year."

"Let's add something new to the show," Lucas said. "I'm wondering if you can pop your head out of a jack-o'-lantern." His eyes lit up. "That would be cool."

"You tried that one with Mrs. Daugherty's teapot," Nora reminded him. "But your head was too big to be hidden."

"Yeah. I'll admit, I need to work on that trick, but I'll get it. It's too funny to give up on it so quickly." Lucas clicked his tongue thoughtfully. "I should be able to shrink the size of my head since I don't really have a skull. There must be a way."

"We can convince Mom and Dad that it's a biology project for school," Nora said with a laugh. She and Lucas were walking past the park.

That's when she saw him.

The soldier in the odd uniform was standing near the slide. The moonlight made his medals shine.

As Nora and Lucas moved closer, he glanced up and waved.

Nora waved back.

"Who's that?" Lucas asked as they crossed the street toward their own building.

Nora shrugged. "I don't know his name, but he's sort of a celebrity, a ghostly legend." She added, "I'm going to be famous too. I bet that someday someone will write a horror story about me."

The foreign man winked at Nora. And then, straightening his jacket, he wandered slowly away toward the next block.

"I'm glad it will be dark by the time our guests arrive," Alyssa Peterson remarked to her sister and mom as they drove down their quiet, one-lane street. "That way nobody will have to see that house."

"It looks creepier than usual today," Amanda replied. "At least in the summer some of the trees hide it."

"I wish the town would just tear it down once and for all," Mrs. Peterson agreed as she turned to pull into their driveway, kicking up dust in their trail. Their last-minute trip to the grocery store for a few missing party items had resulted in bags and bags of must-have snacks. She gently leaned on the horn. A second later her youngest daughter, Anne, bounded out of the house to help unload the car.

The girls were almost finished bringing the bags inside when Alyssa motioned for her two younger sisters to huddle around her.

"Everyone at the party tonight will probably want to hear stories about the house next door, but let's not talk about it," she began. "This is going to be our biggest and best New Year's Eve party yet, and for once I'd like the party to be about us and not that thing next door. Agreed?"

As if on cue, all three sisters turned and stared at the house. The house was something they avoided as much as possible. Its facade was in shambles—glass was cracked on some of the windows, shingles often blew off of the roof, and paint was stripped from the wooden boards that loosely held the house together—but they had heard the inside was even more decayed. None of the Petersons had actually been inside the house, but according to town gossip, floorboards were rotting away, doors were hanging on loosely by rusty hinges, and some of the electrical wiring was dangerously exposed. Judging on the condition of the lawn, it was easy to believe the rumors. An old-fashioned wheelbarrow was overturned and corroded with rust on the dead grass. And a broken light post that stood near the wheelbarrow sometimes flicked and buzzed with a surge of electricity.

The sisters turned back and looked at one another.

"Agreed!" Amanda and Anne said in unison.

"It's almost time, Amanda!" Mrs. Peterson called up the stairs to the second floor. Amanda quickly glanced at the clock on her nightstand and frowned. Her guests would start arriving any minute now, and she wasn't close to being ready for her family's annual New Year's Eve party. She swiped a tiny brush across her pinky's fingernail, adding a final coat of dark berry-red polish.

"Be right down!" Amanda replied. She lightly blew on her fingernails—trying to dry them as quickly as possible—as she walked over to the mirror hanging on the back of her bedroom door for one final chance to examine her outfit before joining her sisters downstairs. The corner of her mouth tilted slightly upward as she admired her new skirt in the reflection. It was a Christmas present from her younger sister, Anne, and to her surprise, she loved the soft pink color. She twirled around and the skirt's light, airy fabric billowed around her. Smoothing down the ruffles, she looked herself over from head to toe, from the slightly darker pink shirt to the white ballet slippers. *All right*, she thought, *maybe I've gone a little too girly.* She slipped out of her shoes and tugged on her favorite pair of silver-metallic high-top sneakers. As she tied the laces, she started thinking about Paul Furby, hoping that he would finally notice her this year.

"Amanda, we need you downstairs now!" Mrs. Peterson called again.

Amanda swung the door open and stepped into the hallway just as raindrops began pattering on the roof. She ran back into her room and peered out the window. Thick, dark clouds hung heavily over their house and stretched out above the meadows that surrounded it. She leaned closer into the window until she could see down to the covered deck below. After lots and lots of begging by the three sisters, their parents had finally agreed that this year the adults would stay upstairs while the girls would be allowed to host their own party in the basement. It would be guys and girls until midnight, and then the boys would leave, and the girls would stay for a sleepover and Mr. Peterson's famous New Year's

Day breakfast. Strictly no adults allowed. And the sisters were hoping the mild southern Texas weather would hold throughout the night so they could mingle outside on the deck too. But as Amanda looked up at the heavy, threatening clouds and saw the rain streaking down her window, she wondered if they were doomed. She hoped this bit of rain would pass soon.

Slowly her gaze swept across the wildflower fields and toward the creepy old neighboring house. And as soon as she caught a glimpse of the dried grass that announced where their meadow stopped and the other house's lawn began, her eyes instinctively darted back to her own familiar deck below. But her thoughts raced to a memory she'd rather forget.

Months earlier, Amanda had been throwing a softball back and forth with Anne, breaking in her new catcher's mitt. Amanda was always far more athletic than her sisters, but Anne was tall and strong and just learning how to really throw a ball. So when Amanda tossed the ball to Anne, she didn't expect her to hurl it back so forcefully. It went straight over Amanda's head and way past their lawn. After scouting through the meadow for the lost ball, Amanda finally found it, and she turned to tell Anne. But when she reached down to pick it up, it had disappeared again. Amanda walked a little further and still couldn't find it. As she walked on, she saw the ball roll out of the tall weeds and into the lifeless yard of abandoned house—as if something or someone was using the ball to lure her closer to it. When Amanda finally snatched the ball up, she was right next to the house, nearer than she'd ever been. She heard whispers coming from inside. She wasn't sure, but it sounded like they were saying "stay away." She ran back to Anne and just told her that she was done playing catch and wanted to go back inside.

The thought of that day still made Amanda uncomfortable. She sighed and decided it was finally time to join her sisters before her mom called her again.

WANT MORE CREEPINESS?

Then you're in luck, because P. J. Night has
some more scares for you and your friends!

Can You Make It Home?

You accidentally stumbled into an apartment
filled with ghosts. Can you make it out of the maze
without running into any ghosts saying 'Boo!'?

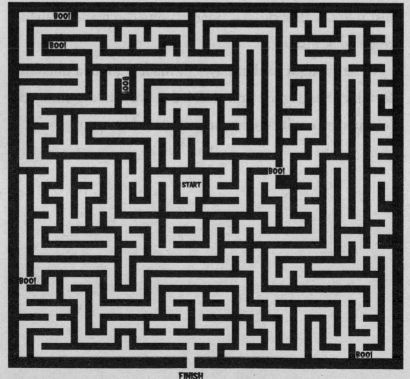

YOU'RE INVITED TO ...
CREATE YOUR OWN SCARY STORY!

Do you want to turn your sleepover into a creepover? Telling a spooky story is a great way to set the mood. P. J. Night has written a few sentences to get you started. Fill in the rest of the story and have fun scaring your friends.

You can also collaborate with your friends on this story by taking turns. Have everyone at your sleepover sit in a circle. Pick one person to start. She will add a sentence or two to the story; cover what she wrote with a piece of paper, leaving only the last word or phrase visible; and then pass the story to the next girl. Once everyone has taken a turn, read the scary story you created together aloud!

I started hearing noises in the attic a few months ago. At first I didn't think much of them, but when things around the house started to go missing, I began to wonder if there was a ghost in the house. I knew I had to conquer my fears and do

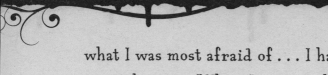

what I was most afraid of ... I had to go up to the attic. When I opened the door, a huge gush of cold air flew down at me, but still I entered. I walked up the steps and there it was. A ...

_____

_____

_____

_____

_____

_____

_____

_____

_____

_____

_____

_____

_____

_____

_____

_____

THE END

A lifelong night owl, **P. J. NIGHT** often works furiously into the wee hours of the morning, writing down spooky tales and dreaming up new stories of the supernatural and otherworldly. Although P. J.'s whereabouts are unknown at this time, we suspect the author lives in a drafty, old mansion where the floorboards creak when no one is there and the flickering candlelight creates shadows that creep along the walls. We truly wish we could tell you more, but we've been sworn to keep P. J.'s identity a secret . . . and it's a secret we will take to our graves!

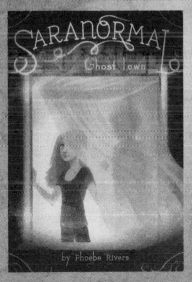